Autonomy of Desire The Novels of Ernest Hemingway

Autonomy of Desire
The Novels of Ernest Hemingway

Rajeshwar Prasad Singh

ADHYAYAN

ADHYAYAN PUBLISHERS & DISTRIBUTORS

New Delhi-110002

Published by
ADHYAYAN PUBLISHERS & DISTRIBUTORS
4378/4B, 105, J.M.D. House, Murari Lal Street
Ansari Road Darya Ganj, New Delhi - 110002
Ph.: 011-23263018, 011-23277156, Fax: 23280028
Email: adhyayanpublishers@yahoo.com

Autonomy of Desire The Novels of Ernest Hemingway

Edition 2011
ISBN 978-81-8435-301-3

Printed in India

Published by Harish Chandra Yadav for Adhyayan Publishers & Distributors, Delhi. Laser Typesetting at Jain Computers and Printed at Tarun Offset Printers, Delhi

To

My parents who not only taught me alphabet but also the language of life...

How pleasant this hour is!
May it extend for me to eternity.

–Anonymous Hieroglyphic Text.

Foreword

Dear Readers! I feel honoured to introduce you to Dr. Rajeshwar Prasad Singh's book *Autonomy of Desire: The Novels of Ernest Hemingway.* Impressed by my credentials and *books – The New Criticism* (2011), *An Autopsy on English Literature* (2010), and *Modernism and After,* Dr. Singh, on one fine morning, gave a phone to me requesting to write a foreword to this book. For some time, I remained a little bit silent, and then consented to do this job despite my busy schedule. And finally, the reading ofthe script yielded a sense of deep academic joy and satisfaction.

Autonomy of Desire consisting of six chapters presents Hemingway's kaleidoscopic view of life in all its subtleties. His mission is to convey a massage which could sustain life and invigorate moral fibre of man for all ages. Against the modern explosion of knowledge, absurdity, and war-ridden and spiritually bankrupt European society, Hemingway explores a meaning of life through the delineation of his protagonist perennially caught in dynamism and incessant struggle. Having a firm faith in human potential and dignity, they assert that man is an extraordinary creation of God, gifted with a boundless energy, a soul, a spirit capable of compassion and sacrifice and endurance. With this spirit of action, they set out for knowing their 'seW-an eternal quest of human being. Hemingway contends that the real self of man gets bloomed when he encounters the antagonistic forces of the world.

He arrives at this conclusion through the character of Santiago in *The Old Man and the Sea* that "But man is not made for defeat." "A man may be destroyed but not defeated."

In Chapter I, "Introduction: A Pilgrim of Reality," Dr. Singh deals with the background material, the shaping spirit, and the biographical sketch of Hemingway. The author also surveys the changing concept of man textured with textual citations right from the Dark Ages through the Renaissance and the Enlightenment to the modern holocaust. Hemingway's concept of man emerges out of action, which is related to his 'self.' The Second Chapter, "Assertion of Self," lays bare the problems of the self of Americans, who are bereft of their roots, tradition, and cultural background and parental values. Being inferior to Europeans and Asians, in this respect, they are obsessed with their real self in relation to this cosmos. There has been a tradition of American novelists who try to assert and explore their true self, now by visiting entire Europe, now abusing social evils and ills, now accepting natural sex life of hippies, now advocating democracy, and now embracing moral values. Of course, the problem of self-exploration is as old as human beings. 'Self is a jewel, a precious one. Hemingway tries to realize man's real 'self in the American socio-political scenario. Once man comes to know about it, his entire problems come to an end.

Chapter III entitled "Sex and Love: Tension of Polarities" reveals that as to how the West is fumbling for peace through sex, wading through sexual degeneration, individual isolation, fear complex, existential anxiety, material luxury, and scientific knowledge. But Hemingway suggests that sheer coupling like animal devoid of love and human feelings is a brutal activity and, therefore, can offer no solace. It will be a mere mechanical and biological function to a restless soul, whereas sex is a supreme action, a kernel of creation, a life force, between man and woman. Sexual act should not be limited to a gratification of sensual pleasure, rather transcend to acquire a spiritual dimension.

But the west has always been ignorant of the significance and mysterious function of sex, which Dr. Singh has evinced through several citations. Hemingway's protagonists always come to self-realization through sex coloured with love, emotion, and mutual understanding.

The author in Chapter IV, "An Encounter with Death: An Advocate of Action and Optimism," shows that death provides an opportunity to realize the true self of man. Hemingway's characters like those of Thomas Hardy always struggle but never yield to the opposing forces. They maintain their psychic integration in the face of invincible impediments of life and achieve a tragic grandeur. Hemingway underlines that Americans should liberate themselves from the fear complex of death. Like Browning he is not ready to cow down before death, but exhibits his adventurous spirit to meet any challenge of life with determination, confidence, endurance, regeneration, and human dignity. In this way, man can overcome the turmoil of human life. Chapter V, "Being and Becoming," demonstrates that Hemingway's characters whole-heartedly accept the reality of life and completely reject illusions and dreams, because Utopian ideals and rootlessness cause alienation from man's own self, engendering existential agony of ' self.' Hemingway suggests coping with the problem of existential anxiety of the modem world in a much systematized manner.

An interesting and informative study of Hemingway's novels, this book deals with his philosophy of action with a comprehensive scope citing a plethora of quotations from the writers of the different languages. The technique adopted by the writer to clarify the concept is par-excellence. Dr. Singh makes a deep study to justify his end. The traditional method of interpretation of a text in Indian academia is generally through the analysis of plot, character, dialogue, setting etc. Dr. Singh rejecting this mode of interpretation adopts a structural method, which will definitely serve as a model to the reader and researcher of literature as to how a text is read and interpreted. His *Autonomy of Desire* reveals the meaning of Hemingway's novels locating them in a particular system. He lays out all the explanations and lets his reader be the final judge.

This book is the most comprehensive review of the dignity and self of man, locating him in different adverse situations and circumstances in the novels of Hemingway. Therefore, it will be used every day by readers interested in death, action, humanism, sex, arid love. The language in the text is easy to understand. The readers and researchers will immediately be benefitted by the book. The author has shown an extraordinary talent to cohere his ideas and presenting them to the reader. Between the lines of the book, his own personality gleams-a serious, disciplined, honest, and a man of few words. Along with Hemingway's vision of man, Dr. Singh's own philosophy of life also twinkles in the pages of the book here and there. Thank you, Dr. Singh, for all your tenacity, resolve, and performing at your very best in writing this book with such a delightful analysis of the mystery of life. Congratulations! This foreword is a stepping stone to the journey of your academic life.

Munir
Professor & Head Post-Graduate
Dept. of English & Research Centre
Shibli National College Azamgargh
India

Preface

With a distinctive literary merit, the growing popularity of the novels of Ernest Hemingway has left a tremendous impress on the reader filling his mind with verve and energy. Keeping this tradition alive, the book *Autonomy of Desire* deals with a very important aspect of his works i.e. the concept of man through the portrayal of the protagonists and their heroic deeds against the social and moral backdrop of the modern civilization. Hemingway has a firm faith in the infinite potential and dignity of man. Steeped in the existential ethos, his vision of life is tragic, but it is never sickening and depressing. It always lends a tragic grandeur exhibiting how his characters eternally fight against the adverse circumstances of life. Amidst the temper of the Lost Generation, this glorification of man shows how death and defeat appear to be standing helpless before his immense power in the novels. Hemingway's idea of death with an existentialist flavour provides an opportunity to realize the true self of man.

The book, in a way, deals with the unique attitude of the protagonists of Hemingway who remain unbeaten amidst actual defeat and death. It evokes a new dimension to understand and evaluate the cause which provides impetus to his men and women to emerge as explorers of life. They never wrestle with any intellectual realities of life but experience acutely a complete loss of faith, violence, bestiality, and death. The book also attempts to show how two motifs dominate in Hemingway's philosophy of action— the matador and the crucified, finally merging in Santiago's epic battle.

The book is structured keeping in mind Hemingway's diversity of fictional oeuvre and treatment of Man encoded across his works. Often the chief motifs are contextualized against a range of evolving perspectives on such notions as the Self. The book introduces a survey on the changing concept of man over the period of time so as to comprehend the reasons which make Americans obsessed about their life and existence. Hemingway tries to realize man's real 'self' in the American socio-political scenario. He underlines the perception of this truth which is eclipsed by human problems and moral malaise.

Against the background of the novels of Hemingway, the reader may look into the West's engagement with sexuality without any inner significance in the modern fragmented and chaotic world. But Hemingway offers the philosophy of sex coloured with love and sacrifice which helps the reader find a spiritual meaning in life. An interesting and informative study of Hemingway's novels, this book deals with his philosophy of action, dignity, and self of man locating him in different adverse situations and circumstances. With a comprehensive scope, the study abounds in quotations from the writers of the different languages and times.

During my stay at Indian Institute of Advanced Study, Shimla, I was immensely benefited by a number of scholars and Professors, who offered valuable suggestions. But the spirited company of Dr. Munir Khan, Professor & Head, Post-Graduate Dept. of English & Research Centre Shibli National College, Azamgargh, showing his positive gesture made a deep discussion on the various issues of the manuscript with his critical acumen. He also stimulated me to pursue my academic life further in the right direction. Truly, despite his busy academic life, he got ready to go through the manuscript to write an illuminating foreword reflecting the essence of the book. In fact, my words fail to express my sense of gratitude to him. I am also thankful to Dr. Uday Kumar, former Fellow, Indian Institute of Advanced Study for showing keen interest in my work. I am indebted to Dr. B. N. Sahay, former Head & Professor of English, Magadh University, who helped me generously in this regard. No less is my overall obligation to Dr. Gupteshwar Prasad, former Professor of English, Magadh University from whom I learnt a lot about Hemingway and the social milieu of America. No less deep is my sense of gratitude to Dr. Aravind kumar 'Sunil' Professor of English, Gaya College, Gaya who offered valuable suggestions in completing this work.

I also owe a special gratitude to Dr. Sunil Chandra Sarmah, Principal, Barama College, Barama who has always been a perpetual inspiration to keep my creative imagination alive. Likewise I am obliged to my colleagues—Mrs. D.D.Choudhury, Md. Zahrul Haque, Mr. Bhaben Lahkar, Dr. Jadab Kalita, Mr. Baikuntha Kalita, Dr. Kamal Nayan Patowary, Dr. Mandita Devi, Mr. Dwipen Kumar Mazumdar, Mis. Banti Ramchiyary and Mr. Biju Pathak—who made my task easy by sharing the responsibilities of the college in general and English Department in particular. I should also mention with gratitude the always helpful encouragement and critical insight of my illustrious friends Mr. Upal Deb, Head, Post-Graduate Dept. of English and Dr. Tarun Kumar Bahadur, Dept. of Economics, Bongaigaon College, Bongaigaon.

However, I am deeply obliged to my father-in-law Prof. R. B. Rai Sharma, Retired Principal, Bongaigaon College, Bongaigaon who always helped me cultivate a style of writing marked with precision, clarity, and directness. I should mention with gratitude the always helpful encouragement and critical insight of my brother-in-law, Mr. Pankaj Sharma, Senior Superintendent of Police, Assam. I cannot but express my feelings to my younger brother, Ravi, for providing me with instant technical facility, whenever required during the period of preparation. I also record my gratefulness to the critics and scholars whose views have been quoted and commented upon this study. Lastly, the loving support of my wife, Era Sharma Singh and my son, Sayan, kept me most of the time free from domestic obligations and made this book come out in this form.

In the end, I must offer my due acknowledgement and thanks to M/S Adhyayan Publishers & Distributors, New Delhi, particularly, Harish Chandra, Proprietor, for accepting my proposal with generosity to publish the book in time.

Rajeshwar

Contents

1

Introduction: A Pilgrim of Reality

The American society of the period between the two World Wars was curious about what the Americans could do and what they were doing. In such a period of self-consciousness, there emerged Ernest Hemingway who preached, as it were, a gospel of action to the new generation of his time. Only work, and intense work, was needed for the regeneration of society, democracy, and other allied activities. In his fictional narratives, he tried to bring home the message in unequivocal terms.

Hemingway's first war-novels were an exception to the American rule of ambitious, unrealized works because he was a finer artist than his contemporaries like Dos Passos, E.E. Cummings and Lawrence Stallings. He began with the idea of war in his first novel, *The Sun Also Rises* (1926), and went on to the fact of war three years later in *A Farewell to Arms* (1929). It was a time when traditional religion became a mockery for large masses of men and the various social elites lost status, and social customs suffered fundamental changes. Like some other American novelists, Hemingway saw the war as a turning away from a virginal and innocent world to a world of evil and corruption, furnished the structure for his first, and in many ways the greatest, novel *The Sun Also Rises*. *A Farewell to Arms* is a fine demonstration of what an artist can do with the naturalistic technique. War was not only violent and destructive, it gave men a possible and workable system of values –courage, and loyalty, and unselfishness. Above all the other human values, there lies the gospel of action without which nothing can ever be achieved in life. Placed beside the novels of the past, Hemingway's novels are slightly cynical and disillusioned. His characters spend their time in drinking, fishing, fighting and wandering. These activities are, of course, time honoured diversions of fictional heroes. In Hemingway, they become not only goals of existence, but also a strong mystical masculine moral obligation.

It is indeed difficult to build anything very solid on such a philosophical foundation. Hemingway draws a touching picture of common humanity in *For Whom the Tolls. The Old Man and the Sea* expresses, better than his predecessors do. Hemingway's faith in the sufficiency of life was unflinching. Old Santiago's triumphant struggle with his fish underlines the moral: to have acted intensely is less enough. Go on working incessantly with indefatigable zeal till the last moments of life.

It is the privilege of every age to consider its predicament unique, and it is its hope that the predicament may prove the most grave that history has known. Such illusions are not always idle: for they are the stuff of which men make the record of their speeding days, heightening their moment with some articulate show of pride, wonder, fortitude, or despair. In the end, such illusions are but the human way of starting: 'We are here!'

We are indeed here, past the meridian of the twentieth century, a devastating war behind us, and a war we dare not call by any name lowering ahead. Yet it is time, perhaps, we called halt to the melodrama of fission and fusion, of grim threats and endless lamentation. Poised at the edge of the Space Age, we have no recourse but to choose life over death, turning our attention to this place, to the actions of man and to his works, which make time and place a habitation for his spirit.

We are here: precisely the cry literature has articulated with the fullest resonance throughout the ages. If that were the only statement contemporary American fiction made, it should have been reason enough to rescue it from the vulgar interest or stylish indifference with which it is greeted. However, the contemporary American novel does not only aver our presence: it explores and enlarges the modalities of our being. To be alive, to be the whole man alive: that is the point D. H. Lawrence wrote with the wisdom that qualifies itself by excess:

> And at its best, the novel, and the novel supremely, can help you. It can help you not to be a dead man in life.[1]

Professors are of the view that the novel is defunct – professors, that is, of their own weary sophistication – condemn current fiction as a spent form, irrelevant to the goals of a Super society committed to a galactic adventure, and therefore no longer receptive to the piteous heroics of the individual soul. Such a view reveals that myopia is indeed the most pronounced trait of utopian vision; and though we can no more refute it than we can refute a nightmare or a prophecy, we can put its judgment to question by inquiring into a more vital matter: the nature of the contemporary self in action and reaction, in stress and freedom, in assent and denial, sallying forth to confront experience and recoiling again to preserve its sanity or innocence.

The action and recoils of the contemporary self engage that dense area of reality wherein our epochal consciousness and our literary forms meet. The movements of the self suggest the regions of tension and repose in our cultural life. Such movements have been the primary business of the novel since the Knight of the Mournful Countenance jogged down the road with fat Sancho by his side. The hero, while life still beats in his fictive heart, mediates between self and world in that imaginative dialectic form we have agreed to identify as the novel.

But what image of the hero does contemporary American fiction project, giving the novel its shape and our world its particular substance? No single answer, of course, will tell the whole story. Still, a beginning may be made by imagining the reactions of a venerable and literate Martian to some current titles -merely the titles -on our bookshelves: The Victim, Dangling Man, The Naked and the Dead, The Heart Is A Lonely Hunter, Invisible Man, A Long Day's Dying, The Color of Darkness, A Good Man is Hard to Find, The End of Pity, A Tree of Night, Lie Down in Darkness, etc. We should not hold it entirely against our visitor if his initial reaction should be that the Planet Earth is on the way of self-demolition. Obviously, a dark impulse of resistance permeates contemporary letters. Novelists are not afraid of admitting it. A Christian writer like Flannery O'Connor and a radical novelist like Norman Mailer concur that violence and distortion must be the means of projecting a vision to which society is hostile.[2] They would further agree that the contemporary world presents a continued affront to man, and that his response must therefore be the response of the rebel or victim, living under the shadow of death.

Such a response goes far beyond the assumptions of mere opposition, and it bears no witness to the charges of neutrality or disaffiliation. The contemporary 'opposing self', to be sure, has the powers of indignant 'perception', has the 'intense and adverse imagination of the culture in which it has its being' that Lionel Trilling astutely perceived in the novel of the last hundred and fifty years.[3] But the contemporary self is also post-romantic. It was not only born, like Little Dorrit, in a prison, and it has not only made of its prison, like Axel, a fortress and mausoleum. It has been also discovering the strange secrets of all prisons: that though their doors are never locked, no prisoner wishes to escape; that all avenues of escape lead to same cell; that nothing may really exist beyond prison walls; that every gaoler is merely another prisoner in disguise. The contemporary belf recoils, from the world, against itself. It has discovered absurdity.

Yet if the American self is in recoil, it is not; we hope and believe, cravenly on the run. Its re-coil is one of the resources of its awareness, a strategy of its will. As we shall have occasion to see, its most tortured gestures of opposition proclaim its involvement in the world it opposes, and its most desperate forms of surrender probe the heart of the religious life in our time. "If the modern temper, as distinct from the romantic, lies in the admission that men are mortal", Wright Morris says, "this admission determines the nature of the raw material with which the artist must work. An element of despair, a destructive element, is one of the signs by which we shall know him -other is the constructive use to which this element is put."[4]

Both elements, we believe, emerge in the new figure of the hero in contemporary American fiction. Precisely what the new hero stands for, no one can yet define. He is not exactly the liberal's idea of the victim, not the conservative's idea of the pariah, not the radical's idea of the rebel. Or perhaps he is all of these and none in particular. Sometimes one aspect of his makeup is underscored, sometimes another. His capacity for pain seems nearly saintly, and his passion for heresy almost criminal. But flawed in his sainthood and grotesque in his criminality, he finally appears as an expression of man's quenchless desire to affirm, despite the voids and vicissitudes of our age, the human sense of life!

It is this quality of his passion, of his awareness, that we have chosen to call radical innocence. Radical, first, because it is inherent in his character, and goes to the root or foundation of it. But radical, too, because it is extreme, impulsive, anarchic, troubled with vision. The new hero brings the brilliant extremities of the American conscience and imagination to bear on the equable tenor of our present culture. His stance questions the 'mystic centrality' of our day, which Richard Chase so ably condemned in The Democratic Vista, and his fate testifies to the continuance of "the vivid contradictions and anomalies that in the past have engaged the American mind."[5] His innocence, therefore, does not merely revert to those simplicities, which, rightly or wrongly, have been identified with vision in America. His innocence, rather, is a property of the mythic American Self, perhaps of every Anarchic Self. It is the innocence of a Self that refuses to accept the immitigable rule of reality, including death, an aboriginal Self the radical imperatives of whose freedom cannot be satisfied. There is something in the quality of that innocence to remind us of the ignoble savage, the archaic and roguish character, say, of the Winnebago Trickster who, as Jung described him,

> "is a faithful copy of an absolutely undifferentiated human consciousness, corresponding to a psyche that has hardly left the animal level."[6]

But the innocence we speak of also has a divine element in it; has, like Dionysus, that inner energy of being, creative and sacrificial, which D.H.Lawrence hoped to find in the American Adam. The disparity between the innocence of the hero and the destructive character of his experience defines his concrete, or existential, situation. This does not add up to an orthodox notion of American innocence – the notion is radical –but it is one, we believe, that can help to make the new hero more intelligible.

Sometimes during the early 1920's, Gertrude Stein, addressing one of her interminable monologues to Ernest Hemingway in her flat at 27, rue de Fleurus, remarked that Hemingway and his contemporaries were 'all a lost generation.' She thus gave a bad name to that group of brilliant writers who appeared on the American scene during the decade following the First World War and who still dominated the American fiction. They included Hemingway himself, William Faulkner, Scott Fitzgerald, John Dos Passos, Sinclair Lewis, and James Gould Cozzens.

"The Lost Generation" is a somewhat misleading name

for them, as a name that reflects the judgment of an the age on itself always is. What this phrase describes is the generation's own feeling that there was almost nothing in the tradition they inherited, nothing in the conventional moral attitudes or political assumptions current in America in their time, that they could accept. They felt that they had to start over again from beginning to work out a code of personal conduct they could live by and to construct a conception of the purposes of American society they could respect. "All I wanted to know", says the hero of Hemingway's The Sun Also Rises, "was how to live in (the world). May be if you found how to live in it you learned from that what it was all about."[7] In this sense, then -the sense that all the maps were useless and that they had to explore a newfound land for themselves - this generation was lost.

It was, however, anything but lost in the sense that it felt despair at the prevalent situation. On the contrary, though it was fashionable in the twenties to talk about being disillusioned, these writers were filled with a typically American kind of energy and optimism. Their scorn of what seemed to them the provincialism of American manners and the narrow hypocrisy of American public life in their time is the scorn of people confident in their idealism. Sinclair Lewis's satiric attack on Main Street may be only partially successful, but not because Lewis doubted that Main Street's stupid provincialism could be defeated. What limits his success is his inability to conceive a cultivated community with which to replace Main Street. It is not despair but hope that creates the dishonest politicians, the stupid labour-leaders, and the selfish businessmen who swarm through Dos Passos's U.S.A. They are the creations of an imagination afire with the possibilities for greatness in American life.

Nearly all the writers of the 'Lost Generation' attacked the defects of the conventional life of their times. It is only lately, in novels, like those of Louis Auchincloss or the most recent work of James Gould Cozzens, that the

American fiction has been able to imagine pre-war America as made up of people no worse –if no better –than they themselves were. But the best writers of the 'Lost Generation' did something more than attack the world they grew up in; they also sought to discover what Henry James called 'the great good place' that they were all sure existed somewhere in the American sensibility, and to learn how to conduct their own lives in order to live there successfully. In an important sense, all good American novels since the First World War –from Fitzgerald's This Side of Paradise in 1921 to Cozzens's By Love Possessed in1957 –are 'pilgrim's progress.' Fitzgerald said of the hero of his finest novel, The Great Gatsby, that Gatsby had 'a heightened sensitivity to the promises of life', and there could hardly be a better phrase to describe the attitude of the writers of this generation. If they were lost, they were lost as explorers are, not as the damned are.

It is possible to see how much the First World War had to do with this flowering of talent in the 1920's. America had perhaps then been a world power for some time, but it was the war that forced the American to recognize the fact that their country was a responsible part of Western Culture. The immediate –and much advertised –effect of this discovery was to make more alert Americans dissatisfied with the narrowness of American civilization to the point where they preferred to live elsewhere. As early as 1921, Harold Stearns performformed one of the symbolic acts of the decade. Having edited a symposium called Civilization in United States, which concluded that there was very little, he moved to Paris. An astonishing number of the writers of the period did the same thing. But the significance of Harold Stearns's act was not his sitting throughout the decade at the Dome in Paris; it was his editing Civilization in the United States. For all these writers Europe was a means to an end, something that would help them discover the possibilities in themselves as Americans.

As long as America had remained, for its own

imagination, a provincial backwater, it had been difficult for most gifted Americans to take it quite seriously. The half a dozen great writers America produced in the 19th century were all -however reluctantly -alienated from their society, whether they went literally into exile, as Henry James did, or only metaphorically, as Hawthorne and Melville did. But the writers of the 1920's went to Europe to discover the American consciousness of experience.

The most significant thing about these writers, then, was their independenly achieved but shared conviction that it was possible for an American, writing directly out of American experience, to produce major novels. When Scott Fitzgerald was an undergraduate at Princeton in 1916, he said to his fellow undergraduate, Edmund Wilson, "I want to be one of the greatest writers that ever lived, don't you?" If this remark was almost ludicrously brash, it was also quite serious, as the persistence of this impulse throughout Fitzgerald's career shows. He clearly believed that it was possible for him as an American to be great writer, and this feeling had hardly existed in America before his time, in spite of -indeed, perhaps because of -the widespread ideological conviction that American democracy was a radically new and in many ways highly successful social experiment.

Young men with Fitzgerald's feeling for the possibilities of American experience suddenly appeared in all parts of the United States in the early 1920's. Fitzgerald himself was a second-generation Irish Catholic boy from St. Paul, Minnesota; James Gould Cozzens came of an old and well-to-do Staten Island family (Staten Island is just south of New York City); Jhon Dos Passos was the son of a successful New York lawyer whose father had been a Pourtuguese immigrant; Earnest Hemingway was the son of a doctor from a middle class suburb of Chicago; William Faulkner came from a backwoods country seat in Northern Mississippi, where his family had lived for over a hundred years. It made no difference. They were all convinced of the special significance of the American experience, and they felt that, by discarding their parents' narrow conception of that experience, they had become free to tell the truth, the private, inner truth, about it.

Their central purpose, therefore, was to define consciousness of experience, that heightened sensitivity to the promises of life that they were convinced was the special product of the American experience. They wanted, too, to learn how to live by the dictates of this consciousness. Because they were aware that what they were trying to define was a product of the American experience, they sought to realize it in the particulars of American life. As a result their novels are preoccupied, sometimes exhaustingly preoccupied, with the minute of American daily life. Ever since the 17th century imposed on Western culture what is sometimes called the Descartian Dualism, the Western world has had to live with a discontinuity between thought and nature, between the inner life of the consciousness and the outer life of the physical and social world. American society was, as it were, invented according to the theories of the 17th century, and one of the results is that the discontinuity between the inner life of the consciousness and the outer life of society is very, marked here. The most difficult problem that the novelists confronted was the problem of bridging the gap between their heroes' heightened sense of the promises of life and the actualities of the society in which this heightened sensitivity was developed and had to realize itself.

Though the other novelists of the period did not emphasize the discontinuities of their sensibilities, as Dos Passos does, by giving each set of feelings a separate mode of expression, these discontinuities are still apparent in their work. There is, for instance, a gap between the passages of Hemingway's For Whom The Bell Tolls that express his own deepest feeling for experience like the death of Sardo, and the passages that present a history of the Spanish Civil War. Robert Jordon's death, at the climax of the novel, is a magnificent image of Hemingway's conviction that the highest form of personal virtue is 'grace under pressure'. But it is almost wholly unrelated to such feeling as Robert Jordon has about the values at stake in the Spanish Civil War.

Hemingway is much more successful when he isolates his characters from the social and historical circumstances that have shaped them, and then suggests those circumstances by his comments on the characters, as he does in The Sun Also Rises. The hero of The Sun Also Rises does in fact learn a great deal about what the world is like by slowly discovering what he calls "how to live in it", what attitudes he must take if he is to retain his self-respect. The first sentence of the book, with their brilliant and subtle suggestions about the character of American society illustrate Hemingway's method in this book.

> Robert Cohn was once middleweight boxing champion of Princeton. Do not think I am very much impressed by that as a boxing title, but is meant a lot to Cohn. He cared nothing for boxing, in fact he disliked it, but he learned it painfully and thoroughly to counteract the feeling of inferiority and shyness he had felt on being treated as a Jew at Princeton.[8]

There is a sharp sense of American social attitudes in those three sentences, of the complex class distinctions of the great Eastern universities, of the exact quality of Jewish experience in upper class American life. There is also a clear understanding of the American concern with athletics. Who but an American would carefully disclaim being impressed by Cohn's collegiate boxing title -as if such titles were as important as those listed in Burke's Peerage -and at the same time suggest, by the evident irony of his disclaimer, the childish absurdity of the American preoccupation with athletics.

Hemingway's The Old Man and the Sea symbolizes man's struggle with nature. Nature, as far as man is concerned, is an amalgam of good and evil. It abounds in giant fishes, which give us sustenance, and sharks, which rob us of the fruits of our toil. The scene in the story is land in the gulfstream off the coast of Havana. After eighty-five days of patient waiting and living almost on the verge of starvation, the old fisherman hooks a giant fish. The fish tows him away into the sea. The old man finds it difficult to manage the situation single-handed. He suffers greatly for the fish badly cuts his hands. It in his nobility of his spirit he does not forfeit his courage. In the face of embarrassing and uncontrolled situation, he becomes religious. The diction in the novel is a web of words, a complex pattern, where the meaning is continually enriched by overtones and reverberations originating from the proper choice and arrangements of words.

It is significant that Hemingway is most successful when he starts from his hero's private sense of experience and moves outward to general social judgments. This method no doubt makes it impossible for him to offer a systematic social commentary, as Dos Passos does in U.S.A. But, it means that the social judgment he offers is in consonance with the book's central reality, the hero's personal sense of experience. In The Great Gatsby Fitzgerald tried to extend this method, and came close to overextending it. In Hemingway's novels, the author is kept as much possible as in the background, except in cases where the author is identical with the leading character.

Fitzgerald makes his hero much more idealistic than Hemingway's about the possibilities of the personal life, so idealistic that he has no capacity for irony at all. Gatsby lives, as the narrator of the novel says, a Platonic conception of himself; he is a man who has committed himself without qualification to his vision of an ideal self; when that vision is destroyed he dies. Fitzgerald has thus maximized his hero's American idealism, his heightened sensitivity to the promises of life. It would be possible to present such a hero directly; he would appear absurd or mad, as

Hemingway's heroes -and even Hemingway himself, who sometimes imagines one of them -occasionally do. Fitzgerald sought to get around this difficulty by presenting his hero indirectly, through a narrator, and by having the narrator provide the irony. He does it brilliantly, but in the end we have to recognize that he means us to be wholly on the hero's side, to believe that without Gatsby's extreme idealism, life is simply unlivable. When Gatsby's dream has at last been shattered, we are told, he

> "must have looked up at an unfamiliar sky through frightening leaves and shivered as he found what a grotesque thing a rose is and how raw the sunlight was upon the scarcely created grass. A new world, material without being real... ." [9]

In the second place, Fitzgerald tried to identify Gatsby's personal idealism explicitly with the social idealism that had been the origin -and was to him still the only endurable purpose -of American society. He ends the book with the narrator sitting on the beach back of Gatsby's deserted house, looking out over Long Island sound and thinking of what it had been like there when the Dutch sailors first caught sight of it there hundred years before.

> ... for a transitory enchanted moment -the narrator thinks -man must have held breath in the presence of this continent, compelled into an aesthetic contemplation he neither understood nor desired, face to face for the last time in history with something commensurate to his capacity for wonder.
>
> And as I sat there brooding on the old, unknown world, I thought of Gatsby's wonder... [10]

This is a brilliant and daring attempt to bridge the gap between the private sense of the possibilities of American life and the public sense of what it is; but the cost is considerable. For all The Great Gatsby's brilliant surface realism it remains a romance, almost a fairy story in which not only the hero but mankind become the unappreciated younger son, the male Cinderella, whose essential fineness is destroyed by and impersonal and indifferent world.

The novel of Dos Passos, Hemingway, and Fitzgerald are the most representative of the period. They are tragic novelists in the sense that their heroes are defeated by a society which has not -at least not yet -fulfilled the optimistic 18th century vision of perfection to which they are all committed. However, none of these heroes ever doubts what Fitzgerald had called his Platonic conception of himself is idealized vision of the personal life. Rather than compromise this ideal, they either die as do gats by and Robert Jordo or Fade Frona the world—as does the hero of Fitzgerald's Tender Is The Night, who quietly disappears somewhere in up-state New York, or the hero of Hemingway's A Farewell to Arms, who as the famous last sentence of the novel puts it, "went out and left the hospital and walked back to the hotel in the rain." For all their practical unsuccess, these heroes are what Hemingway once called one of his, The Undefeated. But they are also the completely isolated. Like the hero of A Farewell to Arms, who made a 'separate peace', they have resigned from society in order to preserve the integrity of their visions of themselves.

Despite the fact that Faulkner's novels are all concerned with what he calls 'The Unvanquished', his heroes have not resigned from their society. Faulkner's 'Unvanquished' is not an individual living by the dictates of his private dream of himself, as is Hemingway's 'Undefeated'. Faulkner's 'Unvanquished' is a community, the community of those Southerners who, defeated physically in the American civil war a hundred years ago, have refused to surrender spiritually. But Faulkner represents this community with all the romantic idealism and sense of greatness that his contemporaries bring to their individual heroes. When Faulkner is dealing with the relation between his romanticized Southern community and the rest of the

United States, it is easy to see how he resembles his contemporaries: in Faulkner's novels. The South is always defeated but unvanquished, exactly as are the heroes of Hemingway and Fitzgerald. But when he is dealing with individuals within the Sothern community, he is a different kind of novelist, because these heroes -especially perhaps the Ike McCaslin of Go Down, Moses -work out in their own lives the dilemma of their community and are indeed almost eponymous.

The heroes of James Gould Cozzens's novels also exist primarily as part of a community, a society that is observed with an insight unrivalled in our literature. The half dozen novels between The Last Adam and By Love Possessed in which Cozzens portrays American communities are the best account of American society we have. Their very brilliance may, however, conceal the reason; Cozzens creates them, the thing that is in the end most remarkable about his work. This is his most compassionate but wholly responsible commitment to reason, to a sense of the necessary limitations of human accomplishment, to a personal dream of life, which is, for all his romantic appeal, a private self-deceiver and a public nuisance. Cozzens's heroes are men of reason, men who have, by an effort of the intelligence and the will, disciplined their own natures to the realities of their society. Their triumph is to learn how to sacrifice their most cherished vanity, as does Arthur Winner in By Love Possessed when he sacrifices his image of himself as a man wholly beyond reproach, in order that the modus Vivendi of his community -a modus Vivendi by no means strictly legal -may continue to exist. The conclusion of By Love Possessed is the climax to all Cozzens's novels, for what Arthur Winner sacrifices is his private - and indeed even secret -image of himself a man of public virtue, and we are made to see this sacrifice as the surrender of the final romantic delusion. That surrender is the conclusion toward which the lives of all Cozzens's heroes since the defiant Dr. Bull of The Last Adam have been leading.

These novelists, then, constitute the first coherent group of novelists in the history of American literature. They were not a school, for they only occasionally influenced each other directly, though personal relations were, for American writers, close. Each had a distinctive voice of his own and a distinctive subject matter. But they shared a common belief in the suitableness of an American experience for literature that was new in America, and this common belief is all the more striking because they arrived at it spontaneously and independently. Americans have, of course, been discovering Europe and Western culture in one way or another since the days of Benjamin Franklin and Thomas Jefferson. But the Lost Generation's much advertised expatriation was a discovery of American experience as a radically different if still recognizable version of the experience of the West as a whole, something that could be accepted without apology or self-consciousness as the material for a great act of the imagination. None of the novelists of the Lost Generation was as gifted as the great and lonely giants of the 19th century American fiction. But taken together, as the impulse common to their generation requires that we should take them, they constitute the finest group of novelists America has produced.

Oak Park, Illinois, is a suburb of Chicago. There, at the end of the last century, Dr. Clarence E. Hemingway practiced medicine. The bearded doctor was highly respected in town, known for his keen eyesight and his great skill at hunting and fishing. His wife, very religious, read the Bible, sang in the church choir, and kept a close, over strict watch on the spiritual life of her husband whom she did not understand. They had six children. Ernest, the second child, was born on July 21, 1899. Relations between his parents, compatible only on the surface, made his childhood unhappy. His mother nudged him towards music, preferably church music; his father put a fishing rod in his hand at the age of three, and a rifle at ten. Male solidarity soon asserted itself. In one of Hemingway's first short stories, we read:

> "Your mother wants you to come and see her", the doctor said.
>
> "I want to go with you". , Nick said. "...I know where there's black squirrels."
>
> "All right", said his father. "Let's go there."

Nick Adams is the hero created by Hemingway to depict himself. Nick's youth is wild and free; he spends his summers in Michigan among the Indians, where he sees life in the raw. An Indian girl, with brown legs, flat belly, hard little breasts, initiates him sexually at a very young age. He witnesses his doctor-father perform a caesarean operation with a jack-knife. He cuts a freshly caught trout into pieces and uses the chunks as bait to catch more trout. His is a savage world of sacrificed animals, such as Victor Hugo knew at his childhood home of Les Feuillantines. And these are years of apprenticeship for a boy who wants to be strong yet has his weaknesses –specifically, an equivocal attitude toward his father. Nick (Hemingway) is grateful to the doctor for the rifle and hunting lessons; but he resents his father's weakness towards his mother and his conventional ideas about 'sex'. Nick's father "was sentimental, and like most sentimental people, he was both cruel and abused .... If he wasn't a coward, he would have stood up to that woman and not let her bully him ... ." All sentimental people are betrayed, "Nick could not write about him yet, although he would, later".

At school in Oak Park, Hemingway showed a fondness for literature and was an editor of the weekly school paper. His schoolmates admired his talent but had no liking for him as a person; they confirmed in him the idea that in life one must be hard, that only the tough-skinned survive. A 'loner', he took boxing lessons and fought so strenuously that he had his nose broken and one eye severely injured. Loving neither family nor school, he ran away twice. For several months, he led the life of a vagrant, coming face to face with violence and evil 'on the road'. He worked on farms, washed dishes in restaurants, and hoped freights: in short, he tasted of that adventurous kind of life 'on the bum' which seems to shape many a young American writer, in contrast to our youthful French bohemians of the Café des Deux Magots or the Café Flore.

In 1917 the United States entered World War I. Hemingway tried to enlist but was rejected because of his bad eye. For six months he worked as a reporter on the Kansas City Star, one of the biggest newspapers in the Middle West. He 'covered' local crime news and accidents. Then he found a way to leave for Europe as an ambulance driver with the American Red Cross. Sent to the Italian front, he soon found himself in the midst of bloody battles in which he served with distinction. He was severely wounded and decorated with the Italian al Vatore Militare medal.

This wound left deep marks on him. He still bears its actual scars along the entire length of one leg. And for a time it scarred his soul as well. He was up in front of the trenches at Fossalta di Piave, when fragments from an Austrian trench mortar hit him. 'I died then', he said. Two Italian soldiers with him were killed; a third had his legs blown off. When Hemingway regained consciousness, he carried the legless, screaming Italian on his back toward a first-aid dugout. As he stumbled on, a searchlight spotted him and a machine gun opened fire. He was wounded twice more, in the foot and knee. When he got back, his Italian man was dead and he himself was close to death. Twenty-eight steel fragments were taken out of his leg.

For a long time he could not forget that hell. He was in a state of shock. He found it hard to fall asleep and, when he did succeed, he would dream of that exploding trench mortar and awake with a start.

> I myself did not want to sleep because I had been living for a long time with the knowledge that if I ever shut my eyes in the dark and let myself go, my soul would go out of my body I had been that

> way for a long time since I had been blown up at night and felt it go out of me and go off and then come back. I tried never to think about it, but it had started to go since, in the nights, just at the moment of going off to sleep, and I could only stop it by a very great effort. [11]

For a while he lived in Chicago, where he came to know some good writers - Sherwood Anderson and his friends. He fell in love with Hadley Richardson, a young newspaper woman, married her in September, 1921, and then left with her to cover the Greeek-Turkish War. Despite his bad memories—battlefields seemed to summon him. There was a morbid attraction to places where there was killing. He saw other terrible things there. After the war he came to Paris, with a letter of introduction from Sherwood Anderson to Gertrude Stein. He could not have picked a better person to learn from.

> "At that moment", he has told us, I was trying to write and I found that my greatest difficulty (apart from that of knowing what you truly felt, rather than what you were supposed to feel, or what you had been taught to feel) was to note what really happened in action, what the actual things were which produced the emotion which you experienced .... So I was trying to learn to write, commencing with the simplest things .... [12]

Gertrude Stein, a massive monolith of a person who had voluntarily expatriated herself from the United States, was a writer with good sense who understood the virtue of everyday words, the power of repetition, and the rhythm of spoken language. These were all the things that Hemingway was trying to master. So a kind of craft intimacy developed between the two experimenters. Hemingway could often be found at Gertrude Stein's house Number 27, rue de Fleures, the walls covered by her many Cezannes and Picassos; sometimes she would come to the Place du Tertre and read through the young

American's manuscripts. He did not write in clichés; he used the plainest and shortest words. She recognized a style after her own heart.

> What was Hemingway trying to say? He wanted to purge himself of violence by expressing it:
>
> "Your psychoanalyst?" "A portable Corona, No. 3."

Hadley Hemingway had a suitcase filled with her husband's first manuscripts stolen from her. It was a terrible blow. Besides, Hadley was pregnant and wanted to go back to the United States, to give birth to her child on the American soil. All was not well with the married couple. Nevertheless, they had a definite programme: 'Have the baby, then return to Paris, and write a novel'. Meanwhile Hemingway wrote short stories. They were hard as nails. One of them, 'Fifty Grand', told the story of a prizefighter who, feeling himself washed up, bets against himself and wins. It was a sharp-edged story, all in dialogue. Nothing was said outright; everything was suggested. Reading it, one is reminded of the best Kipling. Hemingway never speaks of Kipling, and perhaps he never read him. The fact is, a writer rarely talks about the true sources of his inspiration. He mentions those that are the most flattering "Fifty Grand" for publication. Seasoned readers recognized a new master. This twenty-page short story launched Hemingway on his writing career.

After that, all the magazines asked him for stories. The Hearst newspaper chain offered him a contract. Hemingway refused. He was not opposed to the idea of making money, but his conscience did not permit. Above all, he wanted to remain a serious writer, in the Flaubertian sense of the word. 'All I want is to write as well as I can'. To write well, at his own hours –and so no contract with Hearst. As he put it, integrity in a writer was like virginity in a woman; once lost, it was never recovered. Often during his stay in Paris, he allowed himself only five sous a day for a plate of fried potatoes –so he could write solely in his own way and according to his own ideas.

His reputation began to spread among the expatriates. Gertrude Stein, Ezra Pound, and F. Scott Fitzgerald expected big things from him. James Joyce became his friend. Often the two men went out in the evening to drink together. "Once", according to Hemingway,

> Joyce told me he was afraid his writings would become suburban, that may be it would be better for him to get around a little and see the world. Joyce was afraid of lots of things: of thunder, of lightning, but he was a wonderful man. His wife, who was listening, said: "Yes, a bit of lion-hunting would certainly do James no harm."[13]

But Joyce, nearsighted as a mole, was hardly equipped for lion hunting; Hemingway, on the other hand, needed hunting as he needed war. In 1923, Hemingway brought out a little book, Three Stories and Ten Poems, published in Dijon by the Contact Publishing Company. Then there appeared, in 1924, in Our Time, in which episodes alternate with short prose poems, all of them evoking dreadful memories, without comment. Naked, blood-covered facts. Here is an example:

> They shot the six cabinet ministers at half-past six in the mourning against the wall of a hospital. There were pools of water in the courtyard. There were wet dead leaves on the paving of the courtyard. It rained hard. All the shutters of the hospital were nailed shut. One of the ministers was sick with typhoid. Two soldiers carried him downstairs and out into the rain. They tried to hold him up against the wall. But he sat down in a puddle of water. The other five stood very quietly against the wall. Finally the officer told the soldiers it was no good trying to make him stand up. When they fired the first volley he was sitting down in the water with his head on his knees.[14]

Technically, this is excellent writing. The scene is described with cold precision; and its horror stands out all the more against the dull background. Merimee knew that device -over a century ago. The title In Our Time was undoubtedly ironical. It suggested "Peace in our time, O Lord", from the common prayer book. "Peace in our time, O Lord"... when dying men are shot; when crowds insist that bullfighters risk disembowelment; when wounded soldiers groan and bleed in front of trenches; when ropes are coldly slipped around men's necks in prisons. It was a silent protest against violence; at the same time a masochist's delight in describing that violence; and a liberation from it.

> "Your psychoanalyst?" "A portable Corona, No. 3."

The child and the man had seen too much. He belonged to a sick generation, a poisoned generation.

In 1927, Hadley left him for good. He discussed their break, with his usual objectivity, in a curious story, "Homage to Switzerland", in which he pictures himself chatting with three porters in a Swiss railway station, explaining that he is getting a divorce:

> "And it is really the first time you've been divorced?" asked the porter.
>
> "Absolutely ... ."
>
> "And is it very expensive?"
>
> "Ten thousand francs."
>
> "Swiss money?"
>
> "No, French money."
>
> "Oh, yes. Two thousand francs Swiss.
>
> All the same it's not cheap"
>
> "No."

"And why does one do it?"

"One is asked to."

"But why do they ask that?"

"To marry someone else."[15]

Hemingway himself re-married, that same year: his second wife was Pauline Pfeiffer, an attractive editor at Vogue magazine. The next year, 1928, he suffered a heavy blow. His father, Clarence Edmonds Hemingway, committed suicide. Why? It is hard to say. 'He had much bad luck, and it was not at all of it his own. He had died in a trip that he had helped only a little to set.' Now the son harbored a new obsession: Had the doctor become frightened? Fear war destined to be one of Hemingway's great themes.

Heretofore his volumes of short stories, though excellent, had been financial failures. With The Sun Also Rises, a novel about expatriates in Paris -Americans, Greeks, Englishmen -he joined the best-seller list for the first time. His hero, Jake Barnes, wounded in World War I, moves from bar to bar, from shabby hotel to shabby hotel, from France to Spain, in love yet no longer capable of making love. The woman he loves, Lady Brett Ashley, sleeps with a boxer, then with a matador. Brett and Jake suffer -but without talking about it. Romanticism? Yes, in a sense, but a silent romanticism, drowned in cocktails and champagne.

This long cinema-like sequence of hotel nights, dismal drinking bouts, bartenders, prostitutes, and bedroom scenes achieves a tragic effect. Rarely has any human group been so detached from all society. Everything seems pointless. The sun also rises -and just as futilely. The postwar mood of despair was sufficiently widespread for the book to touch the most vibrant chord in "the lost generation". Americans, Englishmen and Frenchmen admired the rawness of the style. This was something new. A

Hemingway novel was to the traditional novel what functional architecture is to ornate architecture.

A short-story collection, Men Without Women brought these qualities to a high point. A short story such as "The Killers" is literally a masterpiece. As Paul Valery said: "You can recognize a masterpiece by the fact that nothing in it can be changed." One enters abruptly into the story -there are no lengthy preliminaries a la Balzac. The reader has to imagine the setting and characters. At the beginning, he does not even know what the latter are talking about. They repeat the same words -over and over again. Little by little the picture emerges from this chaos. What a magnificent story!

Around 1928 Hemingway left Europe and came to live on the oceanfront at Key West, Florida. There he acquired a Paunch, a bread, and a nick name: "Papa." From his first marriage, he had a son John, nicknamed "Bumby". Pauline Pfeiffer gave him two more sons: Patrick, born in 1929, and Gregory, in 1932. Books too were born in those years: in 1929, A Farewell to Arms, a novel about his Italian campaign; in 1932 Death in the Afternoon, a long study of bullfighting; and Green Hills of Africa (1935), an account of a hunting trip in the heart of Africa. War, bullfighting, hunting: "To kill in order to avoid killing oneself." He had to overcome an inner despair, a disgust with human beings, that went back to his childhood. Yet during that same period, Hemingway wrote for Esquire, just as the French critic Taine contributed to La Vie Parisienne. American critics have reproached him for working on such a "slick-paper" magazine, in which his stories rubbed shoulders with erotic anecdotes and drawings. What of it? He liked eroticism, and the magazine had literary standards. Thomas Mann and Andre Gide wrote for it.

Nevertheless, everything seems to indicate that in 1936 Hemingway felt dissatisfied with himself. In Africa, he had hunted with very rich people. He had drunk much, too much himself ("so much that he blunted the edge of his perceptions"). Seven lean years had passed since he had written a good book: A Farewell to Arms. Two marriages had finished badly; he felt that he was being criticized for his association with Esquire ... "He had destroyed his talent by not using it, by betrayals of himself and what he believed in, by drinking so much ... by laziness, by sloth, and by snobbery, by pride and prejudice ... ." In addition, to top it all, the thought of his own death obsessed him. With horror, he realized that "it could all end like this -on an idle safari, haggling with a woman."[16] His second wife divorced him in 1940.

In 1936, the Civil War broke out in Spain. In the United States, many intellectuals enlisted in the cause of the Spanish Republican government. Hemingway was among them. It was less from political conviction than from a desire to sniff the odor of blood again, and to try to believe in something. From this experience came the novel For Whom the Bell Tolls, whose hero, Robert Jordan, personifies Hemingway himself -as previously, was the case with Nick Adams. A hero without political faith and whose sacrifice is gratitutous. Maria, the lovely young Spanish girl, is talking to Jordan:

> "Are you a communist?"
>
> "No I am an anti-fascist."
>
> "For a long time?"
>
> "Since I have understood fascism."[17]

Actually, what were Jordan's political beliefs? "He had none now, he told himself .... He fought now in this war because it had started in a country he loved and he believed in the republic ...." As in A Farewell to Arms, a love story is grafted onto a wartime adventure -but it is love Hemingway-style, sensual, short-lived, and stillborn.

In 1940 at Cheyenne, Wyoming, Hemingway married the writer Martha Gellborn. Together they took a trip to China, and then settled down in Cuba, not far from Havana. In 1942, he offered his yacht Pilar to the United States

Navy and volunteered to serve as a common suicide squadron. He would cruise by himself to attract enemy submarines; then, when one of them stopped him, he would blow up the submarine and himself. It is easy to see why this romantic idea attracted him. The Navy refused, and Hemingway managed to get himself sent to England as a war correspondent. After D-day, this is to say on which a military attack is to take place in June 1944, he made contact with the French Resistance forces and formed a unit of irregulars of which he was the commanding general -or captain. His exact status was unclear. He was "Papa", and the men under him realized in a vague sort of way that he was someone of importance. His headquarters were at Rambouillet. Loaded down with guns, field glasses in a sling, a vermouth on one side and a gin on the other, he proved to be an old hand and adept at war. The Resistance fighters respected him; the army tolerated him. Entering Paris by a different road from the one taken by General Lecture's division, he headed immediately for the Ritz Hotel to liberate it. The symbolism is obvious. At the place Vendome, he stationed a guard at the hotel entrance with a notice: Papa took a good hotel, plenty stuff in cellar ... Then he left for Germany with a division of his own choice. He was a curious war correspondent, always way up in front, calling for tanks to protect his flanks, firing in violation of the Geneva and other conventions, at times threatened with court-martial, at times praised for his bravery.

An American artist, John Groth, described him in the Hurtgen forest. "Everybody knew his jeep. Out of the dark woods you could hear hundreds of voices saying, one after another: 'Good morning, Mr. Hemingway'. It was like a royal progress." Most of the soldiers called him "Papa". Groth tells how one evening, near the German lines, he was having dinner with Hemingway and several officers when enemy shells began to rain down on their command post. All the officers put on their helmets and sprawled on the ground. When the candles were lit again, they saw that Hemingway had remained at the table, bareheaded, his back to the German batteries, still eating his dinner all alone. It was the courage of a man who had known fear and overcome it. He had been through the mill: beneath the mask of toughness, the face had become like the mask.

After World War II, he stayed at a hotel in Venice, where he hoped to write a book about the war. Interrupted by illness (an eye infection which developed during a hunting trip), he gave up that work to write a shorter novel: Across the River and into the Trees, which is the story of a bitter, aging colonel's last love affair, with a young woman of nineteen. The critics weary of praising pounced on this book and tore it to shreds. In it, Hemingway indulged in some digressions on military strategy, in the course of which he attacked Field Marshal Montgomery -hence the irritation of many British readers. In reality, the critics were unfair; the novel was not unworthy of its author. It is not his best, to be sure, but far superior to the best of other writers.

Meanwhile, Hemingway had married for the fourth time. His new wife was Mary Welsh, a Time magazine correspondent. With her, he lived in a house near Havana called Finca Vigia (Lookout Farm). He had chosen to live there because he loved Cuba and felt a little more at ease there than elsewhere. He had had a constant stream of visitors -from Hollywood stars to Spanish grandees. Hemingway, looking like a sacred idol with his white beard, his sun-tanned and deeply lined face, got up at five thirty in the morning and worked. He wrote his descriptive passages in pencil, his dialogues on the typewriter. In the afternoon, weather permitting, he fished with his sailor-navigator. He still believed that the writer must keep in touch with nature by some form of action. If he withdrew from life, his style wasted away.[18] He remained as ardent a fisherman than as when his father had put his first fishing rod in his hands.

In 1952, he proved the truth of his idea that the writer

must keep in touch with life: he wrote The Old Man And The Sea, a short narrative that was received with unanimous praise. After Across the River and into the Trees, someone had said, wrongly: "Papa is finished". In The Old Man And The Sea, Papa was never in better form. It is a fine book: fine in its literary craftsmanship, in its treatment of deep-sea fishing, and in its warm humanity. There is vividness and genuineness of feeling in this story of the old Cuban fisherman Santiago, fighting stubbornly and courageously to land the biggest fish in his life, only to see it devoured by the sharks, who leave him nothing but a naked white skeleton of bones. In this, there is a symbol, perhaps an unconscious one. The giant marlin is the big novel Hemingway thought he would come up with and which the critics tore to pieces. This personal feeling, this smart of a burning wound, gives The Old Man And The Sea its bitter and moving overtones.

After this revenge, Hemingway's war against his time was won. This time the old fisherman kept his catch intact. The world applauded when the Nobel Prize for literature was awarded him in 1954. There could not have been a fairer choice. Hemingway has really given literature a new style, the style of America. At the beginning of that year, for a few hours he was thought dead. While he was hunting in Africa, his plane crashed in the Sudan jungle near the Nile –a region of man-eating animals. Newspapers hastily brought obituary notices out of their morgues. The stories were flattering. But Papa got up a trifle bruised, reached the Nile, and boarded a passing boat. 'My luck is still very good', he told a press conference hastily summoned to his camp in the brush. Thus, near-tragedy was miraculously transformed into a world-wide publicity for the writer.

Hemingway did not go to Stockholm to receive his Nobel Prize. "My wounds, you know." The main reason, however, was that he was busily at work on a big novel. "It was going very well, you know, better than for a long time, when that prize came .... And when it goes well, if a writer stops, God knows when it will come back."[19] But he sent to Sweden a message that was read by the United States Ambassador. He apologized for not being a public speaker. And he added:

> Writing at its best is a lonely life .... How simple the writing of literature would be if it were only necessary to write in another way what has already if it were only necessary to write in another way what has already been well written in the past that a writer is driven far out past where he can go, out to where no one can help him. I have talked too long for a writer. A writer must write what he has to say, not speak it. I thank you. [20]

On the day of the ceremony in Stockholm, Hemingway was fishing off Cojimar, the Cuban village which is the setting for The Old Man And The Sea. He was with Gregorio Fuentes, his sailor, in his black and green boat Pilar, a forty-two footer with two Chrysler engines. The fish were bitting and the sea smiled at the old man. The Time magazine editor who was with him jotted down his remarks. Even if he could, Hemingway would not want to change either his life or his writings. "It's enough for you to do it once for a new man to remember you. But if you do it year after year, then many people remember you and they tell it to their children, and their children and grand children remember and, if it concerns books, they can read them. And if it's good enough, it will last as long as there are human beings."[21] This is the only prize a writer really wants.

"He looks like a modern", Gertrude Stein said of him, "yet smells of the museums". She meant her comment, written at a time when they had quarreled, to be malicious -in reality; it was an involuntary tribute and mark of high praise. A great writer, however modern, is always bound to some tradition. The self-taught person, who starts from scratch, rarely gets far. 'There is no thought which is not about thinkers.' There is no style which disregards the stylists. Hemingway, although a proud writer, read much -if only to go beyond what he read. Moreover, Gertrude Stein herself read and borrowed a great deal from Hemingway and confessed for the same in public. I am not criticizing ; I am simply stating a fact. Who are Hemingway's teachers? He has said: "That's how I learned to write -by reading the Bible." Not only what way:but the Bible teaches the storyteller the art of simple narrative, the power of repetition, and poetry. Hemingway says that he owes much to Flaubert, and it is easy to see what: the sense of discipline, the search for the right word, the need for rhythm in his prose. His is as different from Flaubert's as Jazz differs from Mozart -but all music is music. He praises Stendhal, which should not surprise us. But his real predecessors are Americans: Ambrose Bierce, Stephen Crane, and especially Mark Twain. Hemingway has stated: "All modern American literature comes from one book by Mark Twain called Huckleberry Finn .... It's the best book we've had."[22]

Mark Twain was the first to attempt to give beauty and form to the everyday language of the ordinary American. To Hemingway, the other great American writers of the past are 'colonial' writers, that is, English writers who happened to have been born in America. He recognizes Edgar Allen Poe's skill, "but he is dead". He dislikes the rhetoric in Melville; he cannot read Thoreau. As for Emerson, Hawthorne, Whittier, and company, they were "English Colonials ... who did not know that a new classic does not bear any resemblance to classics that have preceded it."[23] Even though a new classic may not imitate the older ones, it is indebted to them. Hemingway himself is the best proof of that. He observed the simplicity of rhythm, syntax, and vocabulary, which constituted Mark Twain's freshness. But he set his own stamp on these borrowings.

As for his philosophy, it has been suggested above that it owes much to that of Rudyard Kipling -either accidentally or by genuine affinity. The world, which, from their childhood, unfolded to both men, was not a Sunday-school world. Force and deceit dominated it. The hero can do nothing about that: the universe is as it is. Only man, within this world without moral laws, can set up a code and observe it. A code of honour and courage "which, in a life of tension and pain makes a man a man and distinguishes him from the people who follow random impulses, let down their hair, and are generally messy, perhaps cowardly, without inviolable rules for how to live holding tight.[24]

The inviolable rules are not exactly moral rules; or at least they are not those of middle-class, puritan morality. A boxer, a gambler, or a thief can satisfy Hemingway's code, provided that they live up to their contact, which is not made with society but with their chosen companions. 'There is honour among pick-pockets and honour among whores. It is simply that the standards differ.

The capital sin is to yield to fear. One must not be afraid of dangers. Fear comes, most often, from an inability to suspend the functioning of the imagination. Nervous persons are more fearful than those without nerves. There is no crime in that; it is merely a question of human nature. But the code demands that the timid soul must not yield to fear. On this theme, Hemingway has written a marvelous short story, "The Short Happy Life of Francis Macomber". The hero is a wealthy American who has gone to Africa with his wife in order to hunt wild animals. Then, when he faces his first lion, he is seized with irresistible panic. Robert Wilson, an Englishman and professional hunter whom he has hired as guide, has developed a polite contempt for Macomber. The latter's wife, Margot, a beautiful woman, is ashamed of her husband. The night after the encounter with the lion she goes into the Englishman's tent and gives herself to him because he is brave. Wilson accepts his good luck without any outward show of surprise: rich people are crazy, and it is all part of the game.

Mad with jealousy as the unfaithful Margot returns to their martial tent, Macomber feels something happen inside himself. The English guide's solidity and the strictness of sportsman's code, which says that he must not endanger the lives of the native gun bearers or make the wild animals suffer, even at the risk of his own life, leave their mark on American.

Macomber says to Wilson: "You know I don't think I'd ever be afraid of anything again."[25] Moreover, it is true. It is as if his mind has suddenly been cleansed. After all, what can a lion do to you? Kill you. However, a man can only die once. Wilson quotes Shakespeare:

> ... we owe God a death and let it go which way it will, he that dies this year is quit for the next.[26]

Therefore, by a mere snap of the trigger, Macomber has become a brave man -and a radiantly happy one. "You know", he says to his wife, "something did happen to me. I feel absolutely different."[27]

His wife "eyed him strangely." A little later, when her husband bravely stands up to a rampaging buffalo, she fires toward the animal and hits Macomber at the base of his skull. He dies instantly. Was it an accident? No, Margot Macomber, accustomed to dominating, felt that once her husband Francis had become a brave man he would no longer be a compliant husband. So she got rid of him rather coldly, with no risk to herself.

To Hemingway, as to Kipling, woman is both an obstacle and a temptation. She respects the strong man, the man of the code, but she cannot resist the need to dominate the weak man. Captain Gadsby, in Kipling, became both a good husband and a bad officer. In Hemingway's play The Fifth Column, Philip, who has come to Spain to fight in the International Brigade and has heroically carried out counterespionage missions, is tempted by Dorothy, the attractive young American blonde-haired woman.

Dorothy: Philip, let's go away from here. I don't have to stay here ....We could go to that place near Saint Tropez ....Then afterwards we could go to ski.

Philip: (very bitterly). Yes, and afterwards to Egypt and make love happily in all the hotels, and a thousand breakfasts come up on trays in the thousand fine mornings of the next three years; or the ninety of the next three months; or however long it took you to be tired of me, or me of you. And all we'd do would be amuse ourselves. We'd stay at the Crillon, or the Ritz, and in the fall when the leaves were off the trees in the Bois and it was sharp and cold, we'd drive out to Auteuil steeple chasing, and keep warm by those big coal braziers in the paddock, and watch them take the water jump and see them coming over the bullfinch and the old stone wall. That's it. And nip into the bar for a champagne cocktail and afterwards ride back in to dinner at La Rue's and weekend go to shoot pheasants in the Sologne. Yes, yes, that's it. And fly out to Nairobi and the old Mathaiga Club, and in the spring a little spot of salmon fishing. Yes, yes, that's it and every night in bed together. Is that it?

Dorothy: Oh, darling, think how it would be ...

Philip: You can go if you like. I'll draw you up an itinerary.

Dorothy: But why can't we go together?

Philip: You can go. But I've been to all those places and I've left them all behind. And where I go now I go alone, or with others who go there for the same reason I go.

Dorothy: And I can't go there?

Philip: No.

Dorothy: And why can't I go wherever it is? I could learn and I'm not afraid.
Philip: One reason is I don't know where it is. And another is I wouldn't take you.
Dorothy: Why not?
Philip: Because you're useless, really. You're uneducated, you're useless, you're a fool and you're lazy.
Dorothy: May be the others. But I'm not useless?
Philip: Why aren't you useless?
Dorothy: You know -or you ought to know. (She is crying)
Philip: Oh, yes. That.
Dorothy: Is that all it means to you?
Philip: That's a commodity you shouldn't pay too high a price for.[28]

Therefore, love does not exist. Yet sensuality seems to be the very essence of Hemingway's heroes. Physical love, yes; but one must not pay too high a price for it. The modern warrior's woman is one who gives herself generously, between two battles, and knows that afterward she will be forgotten. All she will remember of her lovemaking will be a hotel room, some empty bottles, tips to the hotel cleaners and elevator operators, and some shells shuttling in the night. This is a time of pleasures indulged in on the run.

For a few years, this code was valid for many men and women -in all countries. It was the law of the jungle; the law of a world at war in which fear, courage, and at bottom, despair, held sway. For a time this was the world of all of us; it remains that of a great many among us. Moreover, if we do not watch out, it may well be the world of tomorrow. Its entire morality is based on the manner in which one behaves in the presence of death. In this constant state of alarm, there are two solutions. One is to forget. Hemingway's characters, like their models in real life, drink and make love to numb their senses.

The other and nobler solution is stoicism, which accepts as normal this reprieve for those who are doomed to die. Man walks in the midst of ruins, always ready for the final explosion, trying to forget his nightmares and searching, among the causalities, for "passionate idylls."

> Love, like hunting or war, or drinking, all acts of violence and excess, conceals from us the presence of nada –it is a moment, an all-too-brief moment.[29]

This world is more terrible than that of Kipling, and more terrible than the real world of which it is only an aspect. It is a world where hundreds of towns, thousands of homes, in which hardworking men, devoted women, and fun-loving children live in peace and happiness. Not all human beings need to forget. Obsession with death is a real psychosis –very real –and yet most human beings do not suffer from it. They too deserve to be described. But after two hellish interludes of war, and in the face of even greater potential suffering, Hemingway's anguish is legitimate. This hell is the one we have dwelt in, and in which our children may dwell tomorrow. By contrast, with it, the anguish of a Proust seems mild.

This world is saved by form. To escape 'the senseless of a world without values', there is a finer way out than drunkenness or sensual satisfaction. It is creation. Here Hemingway rejoins Proust. The later sought to surround the simplest things with 'rings of a beautiful style'. Hemingway relies less on images. His style is objective and bare. He describes the worst horrors with classic sobriety. This restraint in describing the monstrous is precisely what style is. As the sportsman makes his gestures of force and skill with grace, so Hemingway –seeking to paint "the darkness at noon" which in his eyes the universe appears to be –has found style as clean and hard, in the words Ford Madox Ford, "as pebbles fresh from a brook."

Above all, to understand the universe Hemingway resorts to vast symbols rather than metaphors – such as the symbol of the old man Santiago and his fish. A world is not wholly without values when it recognizes esthetic values. The writer, like the hunter and the soldier, respects his code; and, by his word magic, succeeds not in recapturing Time -which to Hemingway would mean recapturing horror -but in killing it. It may well be that the world of the universe is nada -nothingness; but in this nothingness, the writer's code and craft dimly outline the shadows of something. Whatever is the point of the narrative, emotional or intellectual, Hemingway prefers to leave it to be bothered from the details of the story. He prefers the method of implication to that of explicit statement.

It is certainly true that criticism of one kind or another has played an unusually important part in Hemingway's career. Perhaps no American talent has so publicly developed as Hemingway's has: more than any writer of the time he has been under glass, watched, checked up on, predicted, suspected and warned. One part of his audience took from him new styles of writing, of lovemaking, of very being; this was the simpler part, but its infatuate imitation was of course a kind of criticism. Nevertheless, another section of his audience responded negatively, pointing out that the texture of Hemingway's work was made up of cruelty, religion, anti-intellectualism, even of basic fascism, and looked upon him as the active proponent of evil. Neither part of such an audience could fail to make its impression upon a writer. The knowledge that he had set a fashion and become a legend may have been gratifying but surely also burdensome and depressing, and it must have offered no small temptation. Yet perhaps more difficult for Hemingway to support with equanimity, and, from our point of view, much more important, was the constant accusation that he had attacked good human values. For upon Hemingway were turned all the fine social feelings of the now passing decade, all the noble sentiments, all the desperate optimism, all the extreme rationalism, all the contempt of irony and indirection - all the attitudes which, in the full tide of the liberal-radical movement, became dominant in thought about literature. There was demanded of him earnestness and pity, social consciousness as it was called, something 'positive' and 'constructive' and literal. For is not life a simple thing and is not the writer a villain or a counterrevolutionary who does not see it so?

As if under the pressure of this critical tradition, which persisted in mistaking the 'artist' for the 'man', Hemingway seems to have undertaken to vindicate the 'man' by showing that he, too, could muster the required 'social' feelings in the required social way. At any rate, he now brought the 'man' with all his contradictions and conflicts into his fiction. If, however, the failures of Hemingway 'in his own character' were apparent to the practitioners of this critical tradition, they did not want Hemingway's virtues -the something 'hard' and 'disturbing'. Indeed, they were in a critical tradition that did not want artists at all; it wanted 'men', recruits, and its apologists were delighted to enlist Hemingway in his own character, with all his confusions and naivety, simply because Hemingway had now declared himself on the right side.

So when To Have and Have Not appeared, one critic of the left, grappling with the patent fact that the 'artist' had failed, yet determined to defend the 'man' who was his new ally, had no recourse save to explain that in this case failure was triumph because artistic fumbling was the mark of Hemingway's attempt to come to grips with the problems of modern life which were as yet too great for his art to encompass. Similarly, another critic of the Left, faced with the esthetic inferiority of Hemingway's first play, takes refuge in praising the personal vindication, which the 'man' has made by 'taking sides against fascism'. In other words, the 'man' has been a sad case and long in need of regeneration; the looseness of thought and emotion, the easy and uninteresting idealism of the social feelings to which Hemingway now gives such sudden and literal expression, are seen as the grateful signs of a personal reformation.

Nevertheless, the disinterested reader does not have to look very deep to see that Hemingway's social feelings, whatever they may yet not become, are now the occasion for indulgence in the 'man'. His two recent failures are failures not only in form but in feeling; one looks at To Have and Have Not and The Fifth Column, one looks at their brag, and their disconcerting forcing of the emotions, at their downright priggishness, and then one looks at the criticism which made these failures possible by demanding them and which now accepts them so gladly, and one is tempted to reverse the whole liberal-radical assumption about literature. One almost wishes to say to an author like Hemingway that he has no duty, no responsibility. Literature, in a political sense, is not in the least important. Wherever the sword is drawn, it is mightier than the pen. Whatever the writer does as a man, he can win no wars as an artist.

Obviously, this would not be the whole truth, yet saying it might counteract the crude and literal theory of art to which, in varying measure, people have been training themselves for a decade. It is believed that the artist to be a man perpetually on the spot, who must always report to people his precise moral and political latitude and longitude. Not that for a moment people would consider shaping their own political ideas by his; but they, who of course turn for political guidance to newspapers, theorists, or historians, create the fiction that thousands -are waiting on the influence of the creative artist, and people stand by to see if he is leading them, as he properly should. They consider then that they have exalted the importance of art, and perhaps they have. But in doing so they have quite forgotten how complex and subtle art is and, if it is to be 'used', how very difficult it is to use it.

One feels that Hemingway would never have thrown himself into his new and inferior work if the necessity had not been put upon him to justify himself before this magisterial conception of literature. Devoted to literalness, the critical tradition of the Left took Hemingway's symbols for his intention, saw in his stories only cruelty or violence or a calculated indifference, and turned upon him a barrage of high-mindedness, that liberal-radical high-mindedness that is increasingly taking the place of thought among the "progressive professional and middle class forces" and that now, under the name of "good will", shuts out half the world. Had it seen what was actually in Hemingway's work, it would not have forced him out of his idiom of the artist and into the idiom of the man which he speaks with difficulty and without truth.

For what should have been always, obvious is that Hemingway is a writer who, when he writes as an 'artist', is passionately and aggressively concerned with truth and even with social truth. And with this in mind, one might begin the consideration of his with a glance at Woodrow Wilson. Hemingway has said that all genuine American writing comes from the prose of Huckleberry Finn's voyage down the Mississippi, and certainly his own starts there. But Huck's prose is a sort of moral symbol. It is the antithesis to the Widow Douglas -to the pious, the respectable, the morally plausible. It is the prose of the free man seeing the world as it really is. And Woodrow Wilson was, we might say, Hemingway's Widow Douglas. To the sensitive men who went to war it was not, perhaps, death and destruction that made the disorganizing shock. It was rather that death and destruction went on at the instance and to the accompaniment of the fine grave words, of which Woodrow Wilson's speeches were the finest and gravest. Here was the issue of liberal theory; here in the bloated or piecemeal corpse was the outcome of the words of humanitarianism and ideals; this was the work of presumably careful men of good will, learned men, polite men. The world was newspaper world, a state-paper world, a memorial-speech world. Words were trundled smoothly over the tongue.

Everyone at that time had feelings, as they called them; just as everyone has 'feelings' now. And it seems to me that what Hemingway wanted first to do was to get rid of the 'feelings', the comfortable liberal humanitarian feelings: and to replace them with the truth.

Not cynicism, not despair, as so often said, but this admirable desire shaped his famous style and his notorious set of admirations and contempt. The trick of understatement or tangential statement sprang from this desire. Men had made so many utterances in such fine language that it had become time to shut up. Hemingway's people, as everyone knows, are afraid of words and ashamed of them and the line from his stories which has become famous is the one that begins 'Won't you please', goes on through its innumerable 'pleases', and ends, 'stop talking'. Not only slain men but also slain words made up the morality of the war.

Another manifestation of the same desire in Hemingway was his devotion to the ideal of technique as an end in itself. A great deal can go down in the tumble but one of the things that stands best is a cleanly done job. As John Peale Bishop says in his admirable essay on Hemingway, professional pride is one of the last things to go. Hemingway became a devotee of his own sill and he exploited the ideal of skill in his characters. His admired men always do a good job; and the proper handling of a rod, a gun, a spade, or a pen is a thing, so Hemingway seems always to be saving, which can be understood when speech cannot.

This does not mean that Hemingway attacks mind itself, a charge which has often been brought against him. It is perhaps safe to say that whenever he seems to be making such an attack, it is not so much reason as it is rationalization that he resists; 'mind' appears simply as the complex of false feelings. And against 'mind' in this sense he sets up what he believes to be the primal emotions, among others pain and death, met not with the mind but with techniques and courage. 'Mind' he sees as a kind of castrating knife, cutting off people's courage and proper self-love, making them 'reasonable', which is to say dull and false. There is no need to point out how erroneous his view would have been where it really mind that was in question, but in the long romantic tradition of the attitude it never really is mind that is in question but rather a dull overlay of mechanical negative proper feeling, or a falseness of feeling which people believe to be reasonableness and reasonable virtue. And when we think how quickly 'mind' capitulates in a crisis, how quickly, for example, it accommodated itself to the war and saved it and glorified it, revulsion from it and a turning to the life of action -reduced, to be sure, to athleticism: but skilful physical effort is perhaps something intellectuals too quickly dismiss as a form of activity -can be better understood. We can understand too the insistence on courage, even on courage deliberately observed in its purity: that is, when it is at the service of the most sordid desires, as in 'Fifty Grand'.

This, then, was Hemingway's vision of the world. Was it a complete vision? Of course it was not. Was ita useful vision? That depended upon one's angle of vision. If it was true, it was useful -if the Americans knew how to use it. But the use of literature is not easy. In their hearts, most of the Americans are Platonists in the matter of art and they feel that they become directly infected by what they read; or at any rate, they want to be Platonists, and they carry on a certain conviction from their Tom Swift days that literature provides chiefly a means of identification and emulation. The Platonist view is not wholly to be dismissed; they do in a degree become directly infected by art; but the position is too simple. And they are further Platonistic a very important fiction. But it forgets that literature in their feeling that literature must be religious: they want their attitudes formulated by the tribal bard. This, of course, gives to literature has never 'solved' anything, though it may perhaps provide part of the data for eventful solutions.

With this attitude the Americans asked, 'Can Hemingway's people speak only with difficulty? And they answered. Then it surely means that he thinks people should not speak'. Does he find in courage the first of virtues? Then it surely means that they should be nothing but courageous. Is he concerned with the idea of death and of violence? Then it must mean that to him these are good things.

In short, the Americans looked for an emotional leader. They did not conceive Hemingway to be saying, 'Come, let us look at the world together'. They supposed him to be saying, 'Come, it is your moral duty to be as my characters are'. They took the easiest and simplest way of using the artist and decided that he was not the 'man' for them. That he was a man and a Prophet they were certain; and equally certain that he was not the 'man' they would want to be or the Prophet who could lead them. That, as artist, he was not concerned with being a 'man' did not occur to them. They had, in other words, quite overlooked the whole process of art, overlooked style and tone, symbol and implication, overlooked the obliqueness and complication with which the artist may criticize life, and assumed that what Hemingway saw or what he put into his stories he wanted to 'exist' in the actual world.

In short, the criticism of Hemingway came down to a kind of moral-political lecture, based on the assumption that art is –or should be –the exact equivalent of life. The writer would have to be strong indeed, who could remain unmoved by the moral pressure that was exerted upon Hemingway. He put away the significant reticence of the artist, opened his heart like 'a man', and the flat literalness, and the fine, fruity social idealism, of the latest novel and the play, is the result.

The Fifth Column is difficult to speak of. Summary is always likely to be a critical treachery, but after consulting the summaries of those who admire the work and regard it as a notable event, it seems fair to say that it is the story of a tender-tough American hero with the horrors, who does counter-espionage in Madrid, though everybody thinks he is just a playboy, who fears that he will no longer do his work well if he continues his liaison with an American girl chiefly remarkable for her legs and her obtuseness; and so sacrifices love and bourgeois pleasure for the sake of duty. Hemingway as a playwright gives up his tools of suggestion and tone and tells a literal story –an adventure story of the Spanish War, at best the story of the regeneration of an American Scarlet Pimpernel of not very good intelligence.

It is this work which has been received with the greatest satisfaction by a large and important cultural group as fulfilment and vindication of Hemingway's career, as a fine document of the Spanish struggle, and as a political event of significance, 'a sign of the times', as one reviewer called it. It seems none of these things. It does not vindicate Hemingway's career because that career in its essential parts needs no vindication; and it does not fulfill Hemingway's career because that career has been in the service of exact if limited emotional truth and this play is in the service of fine feelings. No one can believe that the Spanish war is represented in any good sense by a play whose symbols are so sentimentally personal and whose dramatic tension is so weak; and it appears that there is something even vulgar in making Spain serve as a kind of mental hospital for disorganized foreigners who, out of a kind of self-contempt, turn to the 'ideal of the Spanish people'. Nor, finally, can we think that Hemingway's statement of an antifascist position is of great political importance or of more than neutral virtue. It is hard to believe that the declaration of antifascism is nowadays any more a mark of sufficient grace in a writing than a declaration against disease would be in a physician or a declaration against accidents would be in a locomotive engineer. The admirable intention in itself is not enough and criticism begins and does not end when the intention is declared.

But judgments so simple as these will be accepted with more and more difficulty. The 'progressive professional and middle-class forces' are framing a new culture, based on the old liberal-radical culture but designed now to hide the new anomaly by which they live their intellectual and emotional lives. For they must believe, it seems, that imperialist arms advance proletarian revolution, that oppression by the right people brings liberty. Like Hemingway's latest hero, they show one front to the world and another to themselves, know that within they are true proletarian men while they wrap themselves in early American togas; they are enthralled by their own good will; they are people of fine feelings and they dare not think lest the therapeutic charm vanish. This is not a political essay and the people are not concerned with the political consequences of these things, bad though they be and worse though they will be, but only with the cultural consequences. For to prevent the anomaly from appearing in its genuine difficulty, emotion -of a very limited kind -has been apotheosized and thought has been made almost a kind of treachery; the reviewer of The Fifth Column, which is already referred, cites as a virtue Hemingway's 'unintellectual' partisanship of the Spanish cause. The piety of 'good will' has become enough and Fascism is conceived not as a force which complicates the world but as a force which simplifies the world -and so it does for any number of people of good will for whom the existence of an absolute theological evil makes non-existent any other evil.

It is the group that has made Hemingway its cultural hero and for reasons that need not be canvassed very far. Now that Hemingway has become what this group would call 'affirmative', he has become insufficient; but insufficiency is the very thing this group desires. When Hemingway was in 'negation', his themes of courage, loyalty, tenderness, and silence, tangentially used, suggested much; but now that they are used literally and directly, they say far less than the situation demands. His stories showed a great effort of comprehension and they demand a considerable effort from their readers, that effort in which lays whatever teaching powers there is in art; but now he is not making an effort to understand but to accept, which may indeed be the effort of the honest political man but not of the honest artist.

An attempt has been made to settle the problem of the artist's relation to politics by loudly making the requirement that he gives up his base individuality and rescue humanity and his own soul by becoming the mouthpiece of a party, a movement, or a philosophy. That requirement has demonstrably failed as a solution of the problem; the problem, however, still remains. It may be, of course, that politics itself will settle the problem for us; it may be that in our tragic time art worthy the name cannot be produced and that we must live with the banalities of The Fifth Column or even with less. However, if the problem will be allowed to exist at all, it will not be solved in theory and on paper but in practice. And we have, after all, the practice of the past to guide us, at least with a few tentative notions. We can learn to stop pressing the writer with the demand for contemporaneity when we remember this simple fact that writers have always written directly to and about the troubles of their own time and for and about their contemporaries, some in ways to us more obvious than others do but all responding inevitably to what was happening around them. We can learn too that the relation of an artist to his culture, whether that culture be national or the culture of a relatively small recusant group, is a complex and even a contradictory relation: the artist must accept his culture and be accepted by it, but also, he must be its critic, correcting and even rejecting it according to his personal insight; his strength seems to come from the tension of this ambivalent situation and we must learn to welcome the ambivalence. Finally, and simplest of all, we learn not to expect a political, certainly not an immediately political, effect from a work of art; and in removing from art a burden of messianic responsibility which it never has discharged and cannot discharge we may leave it free to do whatever it actually can do.

Hemingway has enjoyed an unbroken popularity down

to our own time. The secret of his popularity lies in his aesthetic taste. He presented a kaleidoscopic view of life in all its subtleties. He was a pure artist and his mission was to convey a message, which can sustain life and strengthen the moral fibers of man of all ages.

Hemingway was a careful writer who never hurried into print. He followed his craft faithfully. Once he told an interviewer that, "in writing I have moved through arithmetic, through plane geography and algebra, and now I am in calculus."[30] Now, this statement might sound like the arrogance of a man who had become hopelessly entangled in his own legend. But it really exhibits nothing except his fatal obsession with his technique. He spent his final years in depression, culminating in suicide. The fact, however, remains that within his own framework of motive and design; he was thoroughly skilled in the method of his art. In For Whom the Bell Tolls, where he reproduces the speech of the Spanish peasantry, he renders their words in an ingenious translated English, which makes us feel that they are actually speaking in Spanish. Again, in For Whom the Bell Tolls, he shows himself perfectly able to handle educated people whose emotions and ideas are complex. In The Old Man and the Sea, he tells of a Cuban fisherman who is a simple man but not a simpleton. The Cuban's fight with a great fish is in a way an illustration of the Hemingway code of incessant action and in it there is hardly a trace of the sham lyricism that overcomes most writers when they discuss the lives of the Latin poor.

2

The Assertion of 'Self'

The concept of action in Hemingway is related to his concept of 'self'. The gospel of action is basically the assertion of self. It is through active self that the heroes of Hemingway assert themselves in a seemingly meaningless universe. There is a search for identity – essentially an American consciousness. The search for the roots is contingent upon American consciousness. So the search for the self is the saga of action in Hemingway's context. The problem of 'self' is as old as the existence of human life on the earth. The former has remained stationary from the time immemorial. The Universal self of man takes a general account of life of human beings throughout the spectrum of human history. But, the latter has suffered fluctuations from time to time in proportion to the urge and intuition of man to know his place in the universe, the extent of his latent potentialities, value and purpose of his life. It is this urge to know and assert the personal self that is witnessed in the different phases of human history. Mr. A.G. Paranjpe, in his book In Search of Identity, writes:

> Man's search for his place in Nature is as old as human existence itself. We can find men speculating about the nature of human existence in every area

> of human history in all parts of the world. 'Know thyself' has been a common religious exhortation in the East as well as in the West.[31]

What has been pronounced about the problem of existence in philosophy and religion is traced in literature too. Even Eve, the first mother of the human race, has been inspired by the desire to know her 'self'. As soon as Eve is created by God, her first inner urge is to get the knowledge of the surrounding which she is inhabiting. She suffers from an intense obsession to know her place in the world. Therefore, it is but natural that she should embolden herself to go near the tree of knowledge and cast greedy eyes on its fruits even before and she is tempted by Satan. When Satan shows her the gifts of knowledge that she will receive by transgressing the will of God and by eating the fruits of knowledge, she promptly saturates her will. It is by asserting her own will over that of God that Eve asserts her 'self'. Cleanth Brooks writes in Eve's Awakening:

> Thus far I have, I am sure, seem to stress not the human pairs self consciousness -as we usually employ that word -but their consciousness of 'self' ... . This is the only knowledge that the act of eating the apples brings the human pair.[32]

In The Book of Job, the protagonist suffers from an internal obsession to know his 'self'. The sudden blow of misfortune destroys all the members of Job's family and his property. But, he bears all that befall him because he is sincerely and intensely devoted to God. The impulse to know why he is made to suffer, what his real place in this universe is and what his purpose of life is - moves around his act of self-exploration. As he experiences the crisis of personal self, Job also resorts to explore the universal self of man. He says: "Man wastes away like a rotten thing, like a garment that is moth-eaten. Who can bring a clean thing out of an unclean?[33] He cries in the utter agony to know the real self of Man:

> Whence then cometh wisdom? And, where is the place of understanding?[34]

Ultimately, Job challenges God to come and explain it. Since Job is living in a staunch religious age, his urge to know the 'self' of man comes to a peaceful end, when God appears invisibly and rationalizes his doubts.

In fact, there is nothing new about Hemingway's constant theme of 'exploration of self'. All the protagonists of the ancient Greek tragedies are seen engaged in exploring their real 'self'. Oedipus unknowingly murders his father and marries his mother. It is a secret. But the sudden breaking of plague in his kingdom and the prophecy at Delfi of God Apollo that the plague will not abate until the guilty of the murder of Laius is punished, kindle an intense urge in Oedipus to know his 'self' which ultimately leads him to a tragic end. Even the epical hero Odyssey goes from one voyage to another not in search of any new kingdom, but in search of his 'self'. "In a way, the whole problem of Odyssey is the problem of establishing his identity"[35] Zeus says that in exposing Odyssey to Poseidon, in allowing him to go and suffer he is odyssising Odyssey, giving him his identity. In fact, in establishing his identity, Odyssey is asserting and realizing his self. All the Marlovian heroes meet their tragic end in course of their assertion of 'self'. The advent of Renaissance opens a new vista of hope, adventure and inquiry before the people of England. The people now start putting faith in human potentialities. They explore their self by exploiting the human energy to the fullest extent. Before Renaissance, England had been an orthodox country. The people were dedicated to a life of divine services. They believed that God was omnipotent and omnipresent, and human beings were merely His weak creations. Naturally, people neither desired nor dared assert their individuality. With the advent of Renaissance, people freed themselves from the trammels of faith and superstition and came to have faith in individual potentiality. They promptly resorted to different experiments to exhaust all possibilities of human life to apprehend their self in cosmos. Therefore, the Marlovian heroes are seen to be asserting themselves very vigorously. Faustus gained mastery over all the branches of knowledge. Still, he is not satisfied. He feels in his heart of hearts that he has not been able to know his real 'self'. He feels that he can realize his self only by practicing black magic which offers him:

> ... a world of profit and delight of power, of honour, of omnipotence, ... All things that move between the quiet poles.[36]

Therefore, he mortgages his soul to the devil in exchange for his complete mastery of knowledge, and dignity for twenty-four years. This is the intense urge of a renaissance man to know his 'self'. Similar is the case with the protagonists of Shakespeare. They do not want to live a passive life. They try realizing their 'self' by breaking or violating the established norms of their society. Macbeth is a general, unsatisfied with his limited powers. The prophecy of the third witch, "All hail, Macbeth! that shalt be the king hereafter"[37] ignites his desire to assert his self by becoming the king of Scotland. In a bid to assert his 'self', he commits the murder of king Duncan and, thereafter, goes on committing a series of murders. Shakespeare professes the traditional wisdom in preference to the individual assertion of 'self' by showing the tragic end of his protagonists. In the letter Seventeenth Century, and Eighteenth Century, the problem of 'self' never assumed any significant dimension, for the traditional rules and values of society dominated the people. The advent of Industrial Revolution and the publication of the Origin of Species by Darwin gave a fatal blow to the established religious and social values of England. But, by and large, in England there was no tangible trend asserting the 'self' till the end of the 19th century.

But, in the United States of America, during the days of Hemingway, the problem of 'self' became very serious.

America, being a new country with no tradition, no cultural background, has been singularly obsessed with the idea of knowing and asserting its 'self'. The U.S.A. has been a multiracial country with no paternal values. Naturally, the admixture of different influences of different people having different cultural backgrounds, created a very awkward condition. The Americans felt themselves inferior to the Europeans and the Asians. They got obsessed with the urge to know their real 'self'. Therefore, it has been rightly assumed that search of self is the pandemic disease of the Americans. Every American wants to know his real 'self'. They fail to adopt any traditional or religious conception of self as their own, for their rational bent of mind rejects it when they conduct experiments to test its genuineness. Naturally, in the nineteenth century, great novelists like Herman Melville, Hawthorne and Henry James demonstrate the unique inquisitiveness of the Americans that has intensified into a passion to know their real 'self'. Herman Melville is profoundly moved by the intense desire of the Americans to know their 'self'. In his masterpiece, Moby Dick, he shows allegorically an American exploration of self in the fathomless pit of sufferings. He transforms an adventurous story about the chase by Captain Ahab of a white and dangerous whale, Moby Dick into one of the greatest symbols of an American's frantic and lonely quest of unknowable and glorious self which ultimately leads to a disaster.

To Hawthorne, the problem of self appears basically a moral dilemma -what shapes good and evil may assume, how sin has to be understood, whether there is any compensation for those who suffer? It is in this search for the solutions of such problems that the search of 'self' of Hawthorne is implicit. This has been beautifully revealed in The Scarlet Letter. The three main characters of The Scarlet Letter, Hester, Dimmesdale and Roger Chillingworth, undergo severe mental and physical tortures for the sins committing by them without being conscious of their real nature. By committing adultery, Hester breaks a great moral law and disturbs the harmony of a social world. For this, she has to suffer untold mental anguish and live a life of repentance and expiation. Dimmesdale's sin is complicated by his concealment of it. He meets a very tragic end. Though he confesses his guilt in public, yet it brings no relief to him. Roger Chillingworth's sin is altogether of a different nature. His monomaniac vindictiveness dehumanises him and turns him into a devil. Naturally, he pays the price of total physical and spiritual degradation. Thus, Hawthorne perceives that there is no room for the flowering of the self of man unless an over-precaution is taken to prevent it from being tainted by 'sin'.

Henry James, too, is deeply concerned to know the real 'self' of the Americans, though he himself settled in England. In The Portrait of a Lady, the heroine, Miss Archer, goes out to Europe in order to see the world around. She is offered a proposal of marriage by a multi-millionaire, Lord Warwurton and also by a big industrialist of the U.S.A., Mr. Godwood. But, the lady who is in search of 'self' rejects the offers and says that she is not going to marry before she has seen the whole of Europe. A young, beautiful, educated and well-to-do girl rejecting lucrative marriage -proposals merely for seeing Europe, symbolizes the intense desire of an American lady to know her 'self'. This search of 'self' by an young American lady is, in fact, the search of 'self'' by the Americans in the world around. The young lady marries a man, Gilbert Osmond who poses himself to be an artist. (Painter). But then, this man is a cheat who marries her to take possession of the twenty thousand pounds. Archer meets a very tragic fate by being implicated in the fabrication of a cheat who becomes her husband. James shows that the innocent search of 'self' by the Americans has been exploited by the Europeans:

> The Portrait of a Lady unlike such earlier novels and tales, as the Americans, the Europeans, Daisy

> Miller and 'Madam de Mauves', is a novel where the international aspect is so submerged in the story of Isabel Archer's search for the self that one is apt to miss the finer overtones of the problem.[38]

Suddenly, the perspective of the search for self among the American novelists undergoes a marked change. The novelists have been trying to establish their real self in the world. But, the American Civil War during the last decade of the nineteenth century made the budding novelists of the time divert their attention to the American search of 'self' in the American social and political framework. In dealing with the problem of 'self' in the American social -political system - two different viewpoints -Pragmatic i.e., concerned with practical results and Deterministic i.e., which decides the future -developed between two different sets of novelists. The novelists like Upton Sinclair Lewis, John Doss Passos and John Cozzens favour the pragmatic point of view towards the problem of self while the novelists like Theodore Dreiser, James T. Farrell, H.L. Mencken, Erskine Caldwell and Edith Wharton favour the deterministic point of view in dealing with the problem of 'self'. Upton Sinclair attracts the people by his direct attacks on social abuses, which are preventing the poor and ill-paid workers from even knowing their real 'self'. In all his best novels from the Jungle to The Fibber King, he hits out ruthlessly at the social abuses. In The Jungle, he makes his protagonist protest against the incredible working conditions which at that time were prevalent in the Chicago meat packing system. He depicts the annihilation of the 'selves' of the poor Americans at the hands of the capitalists. But, the fact is, his novels always close with the hope that things will change for something better.

Sinclair Lewis projects his own solution of the problem of 'self'. He feels that the present collective, conventional and tribal ways of life are suffocating the 'self' of an individual. In his famous novel, Dodsworth, there is a subtle analysis of a wealthy, American businessman's search for his own 'self'. Sam Dodsworth is a successful businessman. He happens to marry a lovely, capricious and maddeningly selfish woman:

> He feels himself suffocated in the restless and often unnecessary activities of the fellow countrymen and the veneration of God of speed.[39]

On the other hand, he occasionally explores with wrath at the ridiculous misconceptions he finds amongst educated Europeans, that

> "Americans were all money-lenders trying to cheat Europeans or Tobacco-chewing farmers who are likely to split on the Cathedral of St. Mark of Gunmen murdering Chicagon in their beds."[40]

And, yet Europe helps Sam to realize that after all a man may enjoy his life in his own quiet way. In other words, he can realize his 'self' by getting away from the routine of conventional activities and doing something different, in spite of the fact that his best friend tells him.

> You are a typical American in being burdened with a sense of guilt, no matter what you do or you don't do.[41]
>
> Lewis touches here upon a point that as a rule lies entirely outside his usual affair of interest and yet connects him, though very slightly, with that other groups of writers who are more worried about the surrounding in which he lives.[42]

Doss Passos's search of the self is very sincere and profound. In his earliest book of impressions of Spain, Rosinate to the Road Again, he speaks with admiration of the "intense individualism"[43] and the "strong anarchistic reliance on the individual man"[44], to be found in the Spanish communes and of "the conviction that the only individual soul is real."[45] The 'self' of a man is very previous to Doss Passos. He says, in his interesting study of Roger Williams and the spiritual background of American Revolution:

> What we aim to do is to work towards increasing the happiness and dignity of every man, just because he is a man.[46]

Doss Passos feels much distressed at the present social system where honesty, integrity and loyalty result in the complete annihilation of the 'self' of millions and millions of Americans. The people professing superficial loyalty and practicing all sorts of underhand games to gain their unlawful ends have glorified nothing but hollow 'self'. In his triology U.S.A., he shows James Ward Moorehouse as a boy of very modest environment in Delaware, rises through his agreeable manners, his engaging boyish blue eyed look, his art of meeting the right people, using the right slogan at the right moment and a marriage with a millionaire's daughter –to the position of a man controlling almost unlimited publicity in favour of American private capital. He, thus, becomes, according to Doss Passos, one of the greatest dangers of modern society. He saturates his 'self' with an importance which is, in fact, hollow, at the ultimate expense of the underdogs : while there are other characters like Charley Anderson, Mac Williams , Dick Savage, Ben Compton who never get a chance to breathe in fresh air of free life. They do not even know if they have any 'self', and die in utter poverty. Therefore, Doss Passos shows the grim situation of the American social-political system in which the 'self' has no value. In spite of this, he is hopful of some changes.

James Gould Cozzens, in his novels, tries to explore whether the moral values of life can help one in establishing the identity of the 'self' in American society. In all his novels, he depicts

"the position of some individuals in a given setting of life with all its prejudices and idiosyncrasies, men is the problem of adjustment to uppermost the mind of the author".[47]

His novels By Love Possessed is constructed around the central consciousness embodied in Arthur Winner Jr., a lawyer in an American small town somewhere in the east. In accordance with the title, practically all events in the novel are in some way connected with the theme of love in its manifold aspects as a decisive force in the lives of the different characters. The phenomenon of love is in almost every episode placed in juxtaposition with some other principle of human conducts, of which honesty, truth, loyalty on the one hand and social position on the other seems to be the most important. The major events are grouped around on three centers i.e., the hero together with his wife, family and friends, the ill-fated secretary with her brother who turns out good-for-nothing, and the hero's two business partners -one of whom, though reputedly of the highest integrity, has embezzled a large sum of money.

As a result of his experience, Arthur rearranges his scale of values, in which love of truth for its own sake is no longer an unchallenged guiding principle.[48]

Cozzens, here, indicates that unmixed principle of love for truth is not going to make one know the 'self' implicit in the personality. So, in order to realize the 'self', it is essential that new sense if tact and diplomacy should be employed in daily life.

But, the other set of novelists to which Hemingway belongs to reveals deterministic attitude towards the realization of man's 'self' in the American socio-political scenerio. They feel that reality is stronger than man and that human beings are at the mercy of blind forces of nature. It is possible that a clearly stated denial of the existence of free-will would go much against the grain of people devoted to the creation of a new civilization, that it simply could not be made. And yet, the American public have been fully aware that such an attitude is possible, if only as a prolonged mood of pessimism about the status of man within reality. Therefore, the deterministic novelists depict the reality around Man as diametrically opposite to his happiness in the fulfilment and realization of 'self'. Theodore Dreiser is nearer a tough-minded determinist who believes that 'self' of Man is not likely to have any possibility of reaching the stage of complete saturation. The worldly circumstances are such as make human beings completely paralyzed, no matter what way of life is chosen. In his novel An American Tragedy, the hero, Clyde, is faced with the choice between an easy but criminal, and a difficult but honest way of life. At first, Clyde tries to adopt the honest way of life. But, he gets shocked at the utter failure in establishing his identity and recognizing his real 'self'. After his failure to move upward in the social scale, he starts an illicit relationship with a factory girl. Eventually, as he discovers that she is with child and that he could be accepted by a woman of greater beauty and high social rank, he kills her. At the end, he has to be electrocuted to death. This shows that social frustration dominates Man. He has no way out to realize his 'self'. If he adopts the honest way of life, his 'self' will get rot in the worldly ghettos. And, if he chooses a wrong way of life, his 'self' will have to meet a tragic end. Thus, the novelist emphasizes the feeling that the worldly circumstances so much overwhelm Man that he has no option but to annihilate his 'self'.

James J. Farrell, too, emphasizes the same idea of inimical surroundings in the world. In his famous triology, Studs Lonigan, consisting of the novels Young Lonigan, The Young Manhood of Studo Lonigan and Judgment Day, he tells a story of a Chicago youth of Irish descent and Catholic background, his experiences with street gangs and 'broads', in the poolroom and the public park in search of love and a job during the period of depression. He depicts cruelty typical of the naturalistic writer. Studs Lonigan is a very talented man trying to know his 'self'. The potentiality and grandeur of 'self' never come to bloom. There is a gradual deterioration of the hero who, in spite of his talents and decent intentions, becomes the victim of his surroundings, undermines his health by drink and sexual dissipation and finally, at the age of thirty, dies of pneumonia. Farrell clearly conveys the inevitability of the annihilation of 'self' in the antagonistic realities of the world. Other deterministic novelists try to pinpoint the economic and social pattern as the principal reasons for the annihilation of the 'self' in American civilization. Therefore, these novelists are called proletariat writers. But these novelists are not Marxists in mental set-up. They criticize the economic and social pattern for the derogatory effects it produces on the 'self' of the individual. They do not pillorise downtrodden masses. Josephine Herbst, in her novel Pity is not Enough, tells the story of the adventures of a young man in the reconstruction period after the civil war and describes the incredible difficulties he has had with the corruption going around him. Here, Herbst is concerned with the devastating effect that the corruption is social, economic and political system is having on an individual. The 'self' of the individual gets totally throttled by the corruption pervading the society.

A special case, and possibly the most impressive one amongst proletarian writers, is Richard Wright. He has a consistently deterministic attitude and sets it forth in a way that is practically watertight and fearful in its plausibility. There is hardly a better introduction to the status of the intelligent Negro in both the South and the North of the U.S.A. than Wright's work, nor will a European reader easily lay down this book without realizing that here at least is one terrifying problem from which overburdened Europe is free. Wright shows the abusive social and economic system of the U.S.A. which is eating into 'self' of Negro. Elements of heredity, of social environment both black and white, of blind chance and misdirected attempts on the parts of the whites to break down the colour-bar, are brought together to drive the coloured hero of Native Son to the mother of a white girl of his own sweet-heart until he is caught, brought to trial, and sentenced to death. This is the predicament of all the coloured people of the U.S.A., who have no real 'self' or 'identity'. Thus, Wright very nicely focuses the attention of world-wide Public on the enormity of the social and economic discripancy which has left no scope for even the existence of 'self' of the Negroes. Erskine Caldwell, in his novels, depicts the misery of the poor whites of South. In his best-known novel Tobacco Road, he has narrated a very grim and touching story of the life of family of an impoverished sharecropper in Georgia. The family tries tooth and nail to get out of the morass of poverty. They want to know after all what is their real self? Have they been born only to suffer? Will they perish in the world without any taste of happiness or joy? But, utter ignorance, helplessness and depravity destroy tiny chances of improving their situation. In the novel, the man and his wife perish in fire, in the play; the wife is run over by a car: and in the film, the two are sent to the hospital. The fact that ending can be easily changed without affecting the whole is sufficient evidence that determinism of the author is one of the circumstances than of cause and effect. Thus, Caldwell very nicely shows the grim effects of social circumstances, which are bent upon crushing the 'self' of individuals.

Edith Wharton, too, is chiefly concerned with the overpowering effect of social and tribal conventions on the individual. She adheres to the assumptions that the reality of these conventions is stronger than Man who, though he may not always perish in the conflict, will be fatally injured in the pursuit of his self. If, in addition to this conception, the role played in her novels by blind chance is taken into account, the criteria of a deterministic attitude are obvious. The best known and probably the most typical instance of her early work is The House of Mirth. This novel relates the story of a young and attractive woman who, though belonging to New York society, is practically left penniless after the death of her parents. Her plan to secure a rich husband miscarries and the imprudence of accepting money from a man of doubtful reputation proves her undoing. Her friends begin to dessert her and she is forced to earn her living as a millionaire, falls ill, and ideas, a few hours before her one true friend arrives to rescue her. Hence, the novelist is preoccupied in showing bad luck and social-frustration as the unavoidable heart-breaking blows which quash the very 'self' of Man. The fate and social circumstances unite to crush the 'self' of man. Man is merely a tiny tott on the mighty palm of destiny where there is no value of his 'self'. Miss Ellen Glassgow in her novel Barren Ground shows that the heroine is held fast by circumstances as by invisible wires of sheet and has her love thwarted. But, she succeeds materially at the prive of killing her 'self'. Its meaning is quite clear. One can not realize one's real self in the pattern of American socio-political and economic system. Here, even material prosperity is not possible unless one destroys the existence of one's 'self' perpetually.

This was the kind of atmosphere in which Hemingway was destined to breathe. He felt that a new chain of events emerging in the international world gave a death-blow to the established and conventional ways of life, thoughts and ideas. The two world wars stormed the world into a new, ambiguous state of consciousness. Even the stationary universal 'self' of Man got shattered once for all. Human life and human beings both have to be explored in a new way. The American novelists now give up their search of 'self' in the American framework of life. They are now concerned with the self of Man in the universe. Now, a new consciousness grips the subsequent American novelists –the fate of Man. A major part of Modern American Literature grew out of the fundamental question –what is Man? Some novelists tried to probe into the problem of 'self' philosophically, others probe as deep as possible into all the hidden recesses of Man's soul psychologically. But, the novelists like Ernest Hemingway, deal with the problem of 'self'by bridging the gulf between the conception of hard reality and a vision of the meaning of life and death.

Ernest Hemingway, the avant grade novelist of the

United States of America, saw the light in the world in the world, which was the breeding ground of many problems -sexual degeneration, individual isolation, fear complex, and existential anxiety. The hydra-headed monster of problems had had reared up its ugly head and torn all the values of life with unconcealed fangs, in spite of the sustained efforts of the sane thinkers to hold this demon of barbarity in check. The world that has been visioned as a stony universe in The Waste Land of T.S.Eliot, chaotic in The Decline of the West of Spengler and decadent in The Second Coming of Yeats cannot be set in opposition to a genius who, equipped with unbounded stamina and bubbling enthusiasm, is ready to face it. Such a genius is Ernest Hemingway who, though not equipped with the fine frenzy of Yeats, can attempt to diagnose the pandemic American disease and do his best to resolve the crisis of 'self'. A writer with such a noble mission, it is obvious, will have to counter challenges -powerful and crushing. But challenges which threaten to wipe out existence, do arouse creative energy in him, and canalize his potentialities to the creation of something rare and off-beat.

The rapid progress in material luxury and scientific knowledge had severe repercussions on the 'self' of Americans. Though, material comfort and intellectual growth did give superficial satisfaction to them, yet their 'self' remained dissatisfied. This made people revolt against the growing mechanization of life. Naturally, a drive against materialism came into existence and this was called the Happy Movement or Beat Generation Movement. The Hippies came to realize that the very 'self;' of Americans in particular and Westerners in general was getting annihilated by the growing material force. They attempted to liberate 'self' by resorting to free and natural life, as suggested by D.H. Lawrence. This movement does not intend to overthrow traditional institutions, but to observe what Huxley has said 'detachment' from the traditional moral and material convictions. Hippies started living a free and natural life 'sex' life. Kerouace in his novel Subterranean gives the story of a white narrator's love for a Negro girl Mardou in Sans Fransisco. The emotional set-up, it is true, develops along with the usual stages from the first meeting and the first hesitation to the brief happiness of being united, from the first sign of uncertainty to the pangs of jealousy, from the state of being warped up in each other to that of alienation. But, all these result from the fundamental wish to be natural and 'hip'. Though, this free sexual life does give a sense of novelty and excitement, yet, gradually, it degenerates into mere animal coupling. Mr. Winsburg in his novel The Dark Laughter depicts the life of a man craving for emotional fulfillment, independent of material success. He gives up his job of a journalist, leaves his wife, becomes a worker in a factory, falls in love with a woman and, at last, elopes with her. The total impression is that sexual immorality practiced in the guise of free-life is making life repulsive and meaningless. It was initiated to realize the 'self', but it became a game of enjoying temporary orgasms. But, even this orgasm lost its pleasing power. T.S.Eliot in The Waste Land, has given a vivid description of the fast degenerating quality of love, which has been replaced by sordid sex or animal mating. The young carbuncular arrived at the female typist at dusk when she has already taken her meals and feels bored and tired. The lover vainly tries to engage her in amorous gestures. But he has no patience to wait. The suggestion is that the amorous young man hastens to indulge in coitus with the poor humble typist girl at once which accounts to sexual 'assault'. Sex has become a mechanical operation.[49]

Eliot describes how in the modern world there is complete collapse of the deeper spiritual meaning of sex. There is complete denial of the need of discipline in sexual relationship turning it into a source of mere titillation or gratification of the senses. This superficial pursuit of carnal pleasure has resulted in an unbearable boredom.[50] Marriage has now become a mere devise for sexual enjoyment which turns the poor wife into a premature 'hag' incapable of catching the eye of her counterpart husband. The lady described in the poem has turned neurotic. The question in "What you get married for if you don't want children?"[51] is indicative of the vacuity of married life.

Therefore, Hemingway has explored 'sex' in different fashion and has attempted to make it a source of realization of one's self. He makes 'sex' a fundamental unit of life through which an individual can seek consolation in the quagmire of worldly tensions and frustrations, and get the experience of the true essence of 'self'.

The constitution of the United States of America states: "Every individual has an (inalienable) unalienable right to life, Liberty and pursuit to Happiness. "Naturally, individually becomes the very root of American culture. It is for this reason that Woman's Liberation Movement took birth in American soil, for it manifested the will of American women to assert their 'self'. This force of individualism made Americans wanderers. Most of the American works of art emphasize this trend of individualism prevalent in the consciousness of the people. Even the Hippi Movement is the spontaneous outcome of individualism. Though it is a positive trend in a country, which is making all-round progress by leaps and bounds, yet it showed its negative effect too. It contributed to the disintegration of personal relationship, and filial love among the people of different shades and opinions. From sociological point of view, family that is the smallest unit of a stable society began to wither. Everyone started living a lonely and isolated life.

> Beyond all this, the wish to be alone:
>
> However the sky grows dark with invitation cards
>
> However we follow the printed directions of sex
>
> However the family is photographed under the glad staff;
>
> Beyond all this, the wish to be alone.[52]

This loneliness of an individual becomes a torture in

due course of time. This fact has been well presented by Faulkner in his novels. In The Sound and the Fury Faulkner has depicted the predicament of an American family; a father who ruins himself by over-drinking, a mother who is incapable of rearing up her children, a daughter who commits fornication and gives birth to an illegitimate child that grows up to run away with a show-man. One of the sons of the family commits suicide; the other one is a bully, and the third, an idiot. Thus, all human beings are seen living marooned from all human relationships. In his novel Light in August, there is a story of two main characters Lena Grove and Joe Christmas who are homeless, deserted, alienated creatures, strangers on a lonely quest. Joe Christmas has a deep-rooted hatred for his surroundings and is continually worried by the idea of Negro blood. In his restless search for his 'self', he becomes attached to an eccentric lady whom he finally kills. But, Lena Grove, a quiet and stoical woman, seeking the father of her still unborn child, discovers that he is good for nothing and is willing to accept the protection of a well-meaning young woman. The other characters too are lonely figures, such as Joe's mistress who is considered to be a nigger love and, thus, estranged herself from the conventions of her southern family community, the clergyman, a tragic failure in his parish, the facist whose racial hatred makes him the predestined leader of a lynching mob. Heinrich Straumann writes:

> The theme of the whole is evidently that of the uncertain quest of man as a lonely creature for an inexplicable goal, a quest which according to the attitude of the individual will either lead to violence or a catastrophe.[53]

This has made Man a tragic figure. He starts living in an illusory world to off-set the effect of his tragic experience . this is what we see in the plays of Eugene O'Neill and Tennessee Williams. Hemingway, too, explores the tragic condition of a loan man in the world, and shows how an individual has to accept his predicament in a manly way.

The United States of America had no traditional cultural and social values. They adopted science as the backbone of their cultural life. Mr. Dewy, the philosopher who master-minded the educational system of the country, made science the beacon light of American life. It is this prerogative given to science which made the country attain economic prosperity and military might. Abbe de Prett, the chaplain of Napolean, had predicted in 1817, "No human power can stop the march of a nation destined to exert its influence all over the world."[54] It appeared as if scientific values were potent enough to establish lasting peace and prosperity in human life. Edgar Quinet did not hesitate in saying:

> A new idea of God will surge from the lake of Florida, and the peaks of Andee in America will begin a new religious era and will be born a new idea of God.[55]

Thus, an American dream of establishing a world free from tyranny and exploration was born. But, the World War I and the World War II opened a terrible vision of dance of death in its most heinous form. The brutal massacre of human life has been well depicted by Siegfried Sassoon:

> The place was rotten with dead, green clumsy legs
> High booted, sprawled and groveled along the caps
> And trunks face, downward in the cucking mud,
> Wallowed like trodden sand-bags loosely filled,
> And nacked sodden buttocks, mats of hair,
> Bulged clotted slept in the plastering slime.[56]

Horrible descriptions like these about brutality committed on human being made everyone realize that Death as a cruel monster is bound to engulf all, sooner or later. Naturally, the optimism and aspirations of

Americans were dampened by fear-complex. Science was no more recognized as the harbinger of peace and prosperity; it became a merchant of death, for the world wars were essentially scientific warfare. The fear generated by the havoc, created by deaths in war were such that artists like Louis Mac Neice cannot help expressing the deep seated fear of their heart:

> I am not yet born; O fill me
>
> with strength against those who would freeze my
>
> humanity, would dragoon me into a lethal automation,
>
> would make me a cog in a machine, a thing with
>
> one face, a thing, and against all those
>
> who would dissipate my entirety, would
>
> blow me like thistledown hither and
>
> thither or hither and thither
>
> like water held in the
>
> hands would spill me.
>
> Let them not make me a stone and let them not spill me.
>
> Otherwise kill me.[57]

It shows the apprehension of the people that 'self' of man is bound to succumb to Death, no matter how one tries to escape from its shadow.

Naturally, Hemingway comes on the literary scene to preach a new philosophy of life by which the self of man can be realized or relished even in the face of death.

Modern man, with the perception of all the aforesaid nerve-breaking eventualities, has the painful consciousness of the loss of self. Naturally, Americans are seen living a life of wonderer or expatriate, going from one place to another in search self. This 'search' of self brings them close to the existentialists of Europe. Europeans, too, felt that all the traditional values of life have been shattered. Their 'self' has lost its real significance in the world. Sartre, Camus, Becket and others set-off on a new voyage to explore life to adduce some values which mat make the 'self' of Man assume some novel and permanent significance. But, American existentialism has been expounded as "the search for the concrete."[58] In fact, Americans set out in the world to trace some concrete values which may make the people realize their 'self'. This search for self or existential enquiry has been evident in the novels of Nathaniel West, Frederick Prokosch and others. In Miss Lonely Heart there is a story of the agony of a column writer of New York paper who, after several desperate attempts to escape his own professional lies, experiences the collapse of what little is left of the concrete in his world. He tries to find peace in his own interpretation of Christian faith but he is killed by a jealous cripple, when he tries to act upon it. Thus, a sense of nothingness hangs all over the progression of the life of the protagonist. This fact has been more vividly presented by Prokosch in The Seven Who Fled. This novel deals with the predicament of seven Europeans who belong to different countries. All the seven Europeans have different menful set-up and different moral values. But, they experience a common loss of 'self'. An Englishman sets off in an exploration of integrity and loneliness, and at the end, perishes in a snowstorm. The Prussian, in his fanatic belief in discipline, ambition, and leadership, overtakes his physical strength, falls ill and dies after reaching home. The Austrian arrives at a very uncertain compromise between East and West and lives a much-disorganized life. The Frenchman, most acutely aware of the problem that taxes Western Man, desperately tries to disentangle the jungle of thoughts, desires, truth and falsehood, and arrives at a kind of ecstasy of the senses. But, it is at this moment that he falls victim of epidemic disease and dies.

One of the two Russians is all instincts and kills one fundamentally corrupt person among the travelers, while the other is all dialect and has arrived at the conclusion that mankind at the present has only one desire, namely for annihilation. A Spanish girl remains alive by her sheer passiveness. Here, the novelist emphasizes that 'self' has lost its existence in the Modern World because of growing complexities and ambiguities. Paul Bowles has done a commendable job in explicating this existential problem of the Americans in particular and Europeans in general. In his novel The Sheltering Sky, he shows a young couple passing through the periphery of Sahara desert. But, the couple is suffering from some unknown crisis of 'self'. The husband in an increasingly feverish and agonizing search for something absolute who may satisfy his self eventually dies of typhoid fever. His wife, after his death, joins a caravan of a rich Arab, and leads a dissipated life, and goes mad. Hence, in a very artistic fashion, the novelist has shown how the experience of nothingness in life is impinging upon the very 'self' of Man. Hemingway made a revolutionary change in the pessimistic life of the Modern Man by encouraging people to accept the realities of life as they are and to make an honest commitment in life to diffuse the existential anxiety of 'self'.

Thus, the world around Hemingway has been a world beset with myriad problems -sexual degeneration, individual isolation, fear complex, and existential agony -which were annihilating the 'self' of man. The 'self' of man seemed giving way to forces beyond his control. All human actions seem to be fruitless exercise, for they end in sexual degeneration, isolation, death and nothingness. It appears as if

> "... human
> Endeavour fruitless in a world of pain."[59]

Naturally, Hemingway comes before the aggrieved people of the Western world, and explores the sea of life through his novels to a successful end. His major novels, The Sun Also Rises, A Farewell To Arms, To Have And Have Not, For Whom The Bell Tolls and The Old Man And The Sea are different explorations into the reality of 'self'. His novels have become a symbol of incessant struggle and dynamism of human being to encounter the challenges of life with exemplary resilience and realize the 'self'. The realization of 'self' will lead to right action.

3

Sex and Love: Tension of Polarities

> This is the miracle that happens every time to those who really love: the more they give, the more they possess of that precious nourishing love from which flowers and children have their strength and which could help all human beings if they would take it without doubting ....
>
> - Rainer Maria Rike.

W.B.Yeats in a poem entitled "The Second Coming" says:

> Turning and turning in the widening gyre
> The falcon cannot hear the falconer;
> Things fall apart; the centre cannot hold;
> Mere anarchy is loosed upon the world,
> The blood-dimmed tide is loosed, and everywhere
> The ceremony of innocence is drowned;[60]

The phrases 'things fall apart' and 'the centre cannot hold' build up a picture of the universe in which the innocent suffer terribly in body and mind while the warmongers and wrong-doers rejoice. The poet has an apocalyptic vision of a sphinx like rough beast with the head of a man and the body of a lion slouching towards Bethlehem, the birthplace of Jesus Christ symbolizing the rebirth of a new order which will pilot the ship of mankind on the foaming sea of chaos. Omar Khayyam, when he sees the folly of mankind in their act of raising their hands towards heaven for protection, cries out:

> Life not thy hands to the inverted bowl,
> Whom we call the sky
> Scooped under which we live or die
> For it rolls as impotently as you and I[61]

He is so much aggrieved with and shocked at what he feels on his nerves that he likes to retreat to the primal world so that he, together with his beloved, may conspire against destiny to build a new paradise on earth:

> Ah love! could thou and I with Fate conspire
> To grasp this sorry Scheme of Things entire,
> Would not we shatter it to bits-and then
> Re-mould it nearer to the Heart's Desire![62]

Mathew Arnold, too, has experienced the chaos born out of the loss of faith reduced to the night's wind-breath and, as such, he takes refuge into the private world of affections. "Ah love let us be true to one another."[63] Auden's heart-felt realization that a free kiss would cure a million fervers insists people upon taking shelter in private affections. Eliot's The Waste Land which has resulted from animal-coupling and lopsided rationalism requires for its fecundity an unquestioning faith in the resources of soul which, buried in the body, cannot grow, because frost (intellectualism) and Dog (material philosophy ensuring economic security) smother it. To obtain a release from the sharpening of the "teeth of the Dog" or from what Yeats calls "blood and mire", Eliot asks the people to descend lower and lower.

The value adored by the Indian sages caverned in mere alone can guide humanity along the path of a healthy spiritual life. What is the point of concern is that in each age, when established values are threatened out of existence, artists explore new values which can sustain people. This is as truer of Arnold as of Spengler in The Decline of the West or T.S.Eliot in The Waste Land.

Hemingway is a consummate artist of keen sensibility and, as such, he too tries to create new values which may sustain the failing courage of humanity. Restlessness - spiritual and moral -seems to be the legacy of typical American artists like Emerson, Walt Whitman and Hemingway. Each, in his own way, has endeavored to create the values which can serve as a beacon light to the humanity at large. Hemingway, through his novels, has tried to create these values which may furnish the depressed humanity with strength and fortitude, peace and relief.

In a world where no stable value is in existence which may offer tranquility to the restless 'self' of Man. Hemingway, in his novels, explores the human emotions and feelings which may at least make the life worth-living. Modern man is undergoing a terrible physical, mental and psychological suffering. The apparent loss of faith in traditional values is counter balanced by the resurgence of biological inheritance -the craving for sexual gratification. It is, therefore, no wonder that Hemingway should think that 'sex' is an important source of solace to the suffering man. But, sex alone cannot give what society stands in need of.it must be reinforced by love, the kernel of creation. Love orn on the substratum of sexual relation between a man and a woman provides a very stabilizing base to human life and in absence of which life becomes sterile as is evident from "A Game of Chess" in Eliot's The Waste Land. Hemingway discovers in sex the potentiality of renovation and, as, such, he attaches importance to it in every novel. Sex and Love unite to make a man know what his real self is. In all his novels, love born out of the sexual relationship forms the nucleus of attraction. Mark Twain, Aldous Huxley, T.S.Eliot have shown that sex as a means only to the gratification of sensual pleasure has become sterile and barren. No solace or satisfaction can be gained from sex. Hemingway propounds in his novels that if sex remains merely a physical relation between a man and a woman, it is likely to become a sterile and barren experience. But, when sex is tempered with love, it actually becomes a source of highly spiritual as well as physical satisfaction. In The Sun Also Rises, Hemingway has presented the sexual degeneration which has taken place in the present century. One of the most persistent themes of the twenties was the death of love. In World War First, all the major writers recorded it, often in piecemeal fashion as part of the larger post-war scene. But only Hemingway seems to have caught it in its entirety and delivered it in lasting fictional form. In this novel, Jake Barnes and Brett Ashley are two lovers desexed by illusory pretensions. Robert Cohn is a a false Knight and Michael, a man of despair. Except Jake, all the characters are playing the game of sex. No one is seriously aware of the significance of sex. Lady Ashley, having divorced her husband, is engaged with Michael. Cohn who has divorced his first wife to marry another English woman feels gravitated towards Lady Ashley. He takes her away to San-Sebastian and labours under the impression that she harbours deep and genuine love for him. Quite different is the reaction of Michael who, when he discovers Ashley's clandestine relationship with different people, becomes sick of her. His desire to see her constant in love is frustrated. Ashley, in Spain, during the festival of Fiesta, falls in love with a young and tender bullfighter, Romero. Naturally, she transfers her affection from Michael to Cohn and Cohn to Romero in a butterfly fashion. But, in moving from one lover to another, she has her kinship more with Beatrice Jona of Middleton's, "The Changelling" than with the Laurentian heroines who in order to seek fulfilment through sex, change lovers. Lady Chatterly moves from Cliford to Mellovs, because she sees in Mellovs her sexual Mecca. Quite different is the case with Ashley, because she relishes the idea of being a Juliet of half a dozen Romeos. Denuded of all religious and emotional significance, sex has become just a game of lovemaking, an animal coupling of languid bodies and jaded minds. In fact, Hemingway intends to present a picture of a generation where sex-game is a mechanical operation devoid of pleasure and joy.

But, in A Farewell to Arms, Hemingway shows the positive value of sex in human life. Henry is the captain of the army. He is operating on the Italian front on behalf of Italians against Austrians and Germans. He is not different from Lady Ashley of The Sun Also Rises in his attitude towards sex. All the young army officers go to the whorehouse established by the government for the satisfaction of sexual lust. In fact, their sexual pleasure is a mechanical pleasure, and a means to emotional release from tension. Henry, too, thinks of sex in terms of bodily enjoyments. Henry is, in fact, caught in the web of illusion. He is a romantic fool. He thinks sex merely as devise for carnal satisfaction. Hemingway is least concerned with 'whoring' as curse or ideal as Lawrence or Miller is. Miller's ideal woman is a whore but with Lawrence, a whore is not an admiral creature. Lawrence regards prostitution as a profanation of the temple, but with Miller the commercialization of sexuality is not only a gratifying convenience for the male but also the perfection of feminine existence. To illustrate his viewpoint, Miller refers to Germaine, the archetypal French prostitutes of American tourism:

> a whore from the cradle: she was thoroughly satisfied with her role, enjoyed it in fact.[64]

As a matter of fact "She is a whore all the way through -and that is her virtue."[65] Miller points out that sometimes people dare not enter the world of sexual gratification because they either lack courage or stick to false ideals. In his Black Spring, Henry Miller narrates the heroic exploit of his hero, Henry, in the game of sex. Henry pays a visit of condolence to a widow whom he once foolishly reverenced and admired. Stammering and blushing before her, he fatuously imagines she could not be 'had'. Scrupulously, he first sets the scene, welcoming his comrades to the setting of his triumph: "a low sofa", "soft lights" the drink is catalogued and then the dress –"a beautiful low-cut morning gown."[66] Halfway through an eulogy of her late husband, Miller is suddenly inspired "without saying a word I raised her dress and slipped it into her".[67] She does not resent rather she relishes it, as is obvious from her moaning and little shrieks of joys and anguish. Unlike Miller or Lawrence, Hemingway's sole concerned effort is directed towards the liberation of 'self' through sex. In his novel, A Farewell to Arms, Hemingway makes Henry understand the real value of sex and, only then, the real self can be perceived. Within self imposed prison of the self, Henry is unable to connect with or react to external conditions of other people very strongly. His emotional aloofness, when concerned with all others at all, is best described as a pathetically defensive. When the priest asks him whether he loves God, he replies 'no' and the priest continues:

> "You do not love him at all?"
> "I am afraid of him in the night sometimes."
> "You should love him"
> "I do not love much."[68]

The priest defines love adequately when he says that it is not what Henry does or lives at the government-provided whorehouse at the front. The priest says:

> When you love you wish to do things for, you wish to sacrifice for. You wish to sacrifice.[69]

Here, the priest defines love as a commitment beyond

oneself: beyond the unfeeling, unattached conditions of Henry at this point in the novel; a commitment Henry will achieve later on with the English nurse Catherine Barkley.

But, Henry merely thinks love as synonymous with sex. Girls for him are not human beings throbbing with emotions, rather they are safety valves to this sexually changed emotions. He becomes Don Juan incarnate when he conceives of woman as an instrument that can release the tensions of soldiers. He takes the soldier's motto of loving them and leaving them.

> I know I did not love Catherine Barkley nor had any idea of loving her. This was a game like a bridge in which you said things instead of playing cards. Like a bridge you had to pretend you were playing for money or playing for some stakes. Nobody mentioned what the stakes were. It was alright with me.[70]

Henry, imprisoned in his self, goes on indulging in this game of sex not for any real joy but for momentary orgasms. He sees no love in sex and no commitment in so-called love. The priest says to him "you will never know it unless you have it."[71] All the preaching of the priest fall flat on this protagonist. Naturally, he does not desist from engrossing himself in sex as a frivolous pastime. Henry, on a month's leave from the Army, does not go to the cold, clear and dry mountain where the priest invited him to stay with his family during leave. Henry goes to the place and observes:

> Smock of cafes and nights where the room whirled and you need not lack at the wall to make it stop, nights in bed, drink, where he knew that was all there was-and the world unreal in the dark sure that this was all and all and not caring."[72]

Following his thoughts about pretention in love, he insits that Catherine should kiss him. This has been presented with the help of contrasts carefully woven in the pattern of the following paragraph:

> We kissed and she broke away suddenly. No, Good-night, please-darling. We walked to door and I saw her go in and down the hall. I went on home. It was a hot night and there was a good deal going on up in the mountain. I watched flashes on San Gabriele.[73]

Catherine has recently lost in the war with the man she was going to marry. She has been deeply wounded emotionally and her sudden outbursts and changes of behavior cause Henry to think of her, rather dispassionately as a little crazy. It is obvious to the reader that she is extremely vulnerable and a good deal more involved in the relationship than Henry is. In the paragraph cited above, her emotional withdrawal from the situation that she knows she is already committed to sharp contrasts with Henry's casual impersonality. Henry has failed to recognize that something more is going to evolve from their relationship. His apparent sexual attraction for Catherine tends to develop into deep 'love'. Henry remains indifferent to this fact. But, when he gets mortally wounded by the mortar-shell on the Italian front, his heroic attitude towards war gradually melts and his 'love' for Catherine gradually emerges. When he is admitted to the hospital of Milan, he gets a chance to live with Catherine for a long time. Now, he comes to understand that the physical relationship with Catherine has given rise to something which is much higher and purer than he used to suppose. He now thinks much more about the welfare of Catherine than about himself. Now, he is in real love. He has also made a commitment, a commitment beyond himself, and in this commitment, he realizes his real self. But, Hemingway very clearly demonstrates that this love which seems to irradiate his being feeds on sex. The novelist very graphically traces the effect of love. Henry, who has a gradual realization of the forces of love in himself feels:

> God knows I had wanted to fall in love with anyone. I had not wanted to fall in love with anyone. But, God knows I had and I lay on the bed in the room of the hospital in Milan and all sorts of thing went through any head but I felt wonderful.[74]

It is the intensity of love which makes them think that they are a married couple although they have not been married in church. What is that which makes them think that they are husband and wife? The positive answer to this question lies in the fact that they are padlocked into love, though not in wedlock. Naturally, Henry becomes unnerved and excited when he comes to know that Catherine is pregnant. To externalize his latent emotions, he desires to celebrate his marriage with Catherine in the church. This desire of Henry cannot be attributed to social fear. He is anxious because Catherine will feel awkward if people will come to know about her pregnancy. This reminds us of Shakespeare's Measure for Measure in which Claudio, the protagonist, is least concerned with the social infamy which the pregnancy of Juliet, his beloved will bring. There can be no gainsaying the truth that Claudio fears death-sentence but is apathetic to social infamy. Quite different is the case with Henry, the protagonist of Hemingway's novel A Farewell to Arms who, as he loves Catherine deeply, cannot bear the idea that his beloved should be mortified with a sense of pain, because of her pregnancy before her marriage in the church. Therefore, he frantically personates Catherine for marriage. But, Catherine knows that what matters is love. Marriage may be a social guarantee but it does not promise any 'love' between the partners. Therefore, she is ready to bear the child of love instead of any so-called issue of marriage formalities. So when Henry says:

> 'I only wanted it for you'.
> 'I am not any me. I am you'
> 'Don't make up a separate me.'
> 'I thought girls always wanted to be married.'

'They do. But darling, I am married. I am married to you. Don't I make you a good wife?'
'You are a lovely wife!'[75]

The conversation between Henry and Catherine points to the fact that true marriage is the marriage of minds, of the fusion of two bodies in one. Where there is the complete fusion of two bodies in one, there is no need for the celebration of matrimonial formalities. She, therefore, thinks that she is married. Through the conversation between these two characters, Hemingway has launched a violent attack on the matrimonial ceremonies tinctured round by what Richardson calls calico purity. Lawrence does not favour the observance of matrimonial ceremonies. He does not favour the fusion of two bodies either, although he stresses the significance of real union of man and woman in life. His concept of 'divine otherness' is illustrative of this truth and the violation of which sows the seeds of tragedy in human life as is evident from the thematic pattern of Sons and Lovers.

Hemingway does not like Lawrence to attach any mystical significance to sex nor does he advocate the violation of the established social code. What he intends to present in his novels is that if the established values fail to engage the faith of the people, people can live and live by the emergence of new values unity in duality – "I am not any me, I am you." It is patent that Henry and Catherine have made a commitment beyond themselves and this is the real 'self' of Henry. The real 'self' of Man becomes clear not in being always engrossed in one's own benefit and profit, it becomes perceptible in the process of self-effacement for a commitment made to another in 'love'; this love is the product of pure physical relation between man and woman. Henry becomes even more conscious of the beauty of 'love' when the Italian army suffers a humiliating defeat at the hands of the Germans, and has to beat a hasty retreat. The horrors and brutality of war shatter the romantic longings of Henry. The breaking of Henry's glorious dream about wars brings to our mind the picture of Sergius who, after the shattering of his romantic notions of war, has the realization that soldiering is the coward's art of attacking enemy mercilessly when the enemy is weak and keeping out of the harm's way when the enemy is strong. "Oh, war! war! the dream of patriots and heroes! A fraud, Bluntschli. A hallow sham."[76] When Henry is retreating with his friend from the front, he gets more and more conscious of his 'love' for Catherine. He keeps on speculating how Catherine manages to give birth to the 'baby'. He sees that the Italian guardsmen are shooting down without rhyme or reason those Italian officers who are retreating from the front. He makes a miraculous escape by diving in a neighboring river. But, all the time, his mind is haunted by the memory of Catherine and he crosses the border lying on the cool floor of the cabin of a train. He is wet. But, even in this uncomfortable condition, he gets completely absorbed in thinking about Catherine:

> I could remember Catherine but I knew I would get crazy if I thought her when I was not seen yet I would see her, so I would not think about her, only about her a little, only about her with the car going slowly and chickingly, and some light through the canvass and my lying with Catherine on the floor of the car to lie not thinking only feeling, having been away too long, the cloth wet and floor moving only a little each time and lone -some inside and alone with wet clothing and hard floor for a wife.[77]

Hemingway clearly shows that even in the teeth of danger and death, the 'self' of Henry remains pacified and joyful at the prospect of his union with Catherine. Buoyed with new hope, he manages to escape. Hours that he spends in the company of Catherine revitalize him. To his shock and surprise, he comes to know that the military police are on their way to arrest him for desertion. He and Catherine sneak out of the hotel and row across the lake to Switzerland. But, Switzerland does not remain a dreamland for ever, because 'Love' is also bound to meet the same fate as the other things of the world meet. In Henry's movement towards full commitment to Catherine, there is accompanying growth of what has been called 'the sense of doom'. Catherine dies while giving birth to a baby and the baby is a stillborn baby. Henry, without being sentimental goes into the hospital. The fact is, he made a commitment and that commitment is fulfilled. Thus, the 'self' of Henry stands confident, aware and pacified. Hemingway knows that 'sex' and 'love' are the two ingredients that give a very distinct identity to the 'self' of Man. Though it is not a perpetual possession, yet it contributes in a lrge measure to self-realization. Therefore,

> For Hemingway, sex is an essential ingredient in love between man and woman, and the continuation of Catherine and Henry's sexual relationship throughout a summer is the medium by which true regard for the person is reached.[78]

This true regard develops into a love in which a sense of sacrifice and selflessness emerge in the heart, and this is the real self of Man.

The novel presents a movement from the world of war to the world of dream and romance. The drift of the chief protagonist from the world of sickening cruelty, which reminds him of the omnipotence of death to the dream world of his love, is necessitated by his perception that love is the only way in which man can overcome his loneliness. It is thus quite clear that Hemingway's hero, like Arnold of Dover Beach, tries to seek in the private world of affections and understanding of his 'self'. There is no denying the truth that Henry deludes himself about the power of love. By fleeing the battlefield and making his separate peace, he cannot evade death completely but he has the courage to "meet that tragedy with dignity and stoical endurance."[79] All that Henry has developed has been possible through his commitment to the cause of love and sex.

In To Have and Have Not, Hemingway has presented the struggling life of Harry Morgan. He has to resort to smuggling and other anti-social ways under pressure of social circumstances. But, Harry goes on encountering all the worldly obstacles and suffering with full confidence. He loses his left arm in this sort of life. Still, without being least disappointed, he goes on struggling against the untoward circumstances of his life. Harry is a lone figure. There is no one to give any relief to his agonized soul. But, sex is the only source which gives him some sort of relief. It is during the sexual affair with his wife that he experiences a moment of diversion from the hectic life he leads. The only person who ever engages his care and attention is his wife. Thus, sex and love born of this sex are the only two factors which contribute to the happiness of Harry Morgan. The given dialogues between his wife and Harry are the only moments in which the latter appears to be free from all mental tension and anxiety:

> 'I don't want to wait. Come on. That's it.'
>
> 'That's where, listen, did you ever do it with a nigger wench?'
>
> 'Sure'
>
> 'What's it like?'
>
> 'Like nurse shark.'
>
> "You're funny. Harry, I with you didn't have to go. I wish you didn't ever have to go. Who is the best you ever did it wish?'
>
> 'You'.
>
> 'You. You always lie to me.
>
> There. There. There.'

'No, you're the best.'

'I'm old.'

'You'ill never be old'.

'I've had that thig.'

'That don't make no difference when a woman's any good'.[80]

The love which he gets from his wife reinforces him with vital springs of joy and equips him with capacity to face the hazards of life with confidence and enthusiasm. Harry dies by the gun-shot that he receives in his abdomen while killing the gangsters on his boat. But, even when he is dying, there is only one conflict obsessing his mind:

It's crowded, he thought. That's what it is, it's crowded. Then, he thought, I wonder what she'ill do. I wonder what Marie will do? May be they'ill pay her the rewards. God damn that Cuban. She'ill get along, I guess. She's a smart woman. I guess we could all have gotten along. I guess it was nuts all right. I guess I bit off too much more than I could chew. I shouldn't have tried it. I had it all right up to the end. Nobody'll know how it happened. I wish I could do something about Marie.[81]

Thus, even in this novel, the value of sex as force that can rejuvenate the self has been emphasized by Hemingway.

In For Whom the Bell Tolls, Hemingway highlights the significance of sex in the revitalization of the self. In the novel, the hero, Jordon, an American, has to take the risk of blowing a bridge with Guerillas inhabiting a neighboring mountain. He is aware that he may lose his life in executing this operation, yet he does not lose his heart even for a minute. Jordan meets Maria who feels her 'self' disintegrated on account of mass rape committed upon her by fascists. Naturally, she is incapable of seeing in love the creative energy that makes life worth living. Pilar tries to instill confidence and power in her so that she may assert her 'self'. Therefore, she sends her to Jordon.

She feels that by the sexual pleasure and joy, her identity may be rejuvenated. Therefore, when Jordon and Maria meet each other at night, the sexual affair between them reactivates a sense of novel self in her heart. Thus, it is the sexual power which revives the frozen self of Maria. She says:

> I loved you, when I saw you today and I love you always but never saw you before and I told Pilar.... Now I am happy that I did not die. [82]

Sex revives her 'self'. Her implicit assertion of self is revealed in her desire to have sexual pleasure with Jordon and her intense effort to show love to him.

> "And now let us do quickly what it is weds so that the other is all gone."
>
> "You want"
>
> "Yes", she said almost fiercely "Yes, yes, yes."[83]

Now, her self is being asserted. It is no more dormant. It revives a new love of life in her.

Jordon, too, is somewhat tired with his hard and tough work. The chance to have sexual relation with Maria provides him not only physical sensation, but also a sense of profound relief. It is a solution to his mental puzzle and a relief from his physical exertion. In other words, sex gives a miraculous relief to his fatigued body and soul. He starts thinking afresh about the plans of blowing up the bridge, in a more concrete and practical manner. He feels very light and energetic. Maria, Jordan and Pilar go to meet Sordo at his residence which is on the other part of the hill. Pilar leaves the two all alone at the retreat. Here, Maria and Jordon are favoured with a chance to renew their vitality through the process of sexual intercourse. But now, this sex assumes a new and vital significance. The pleasure of the sexual encounter comes very near to mystical experience. They get united not only physically, but also spiritually. Jordon had affairs with many other young women but those sexual intercourses gave only momentary pleasure like the experiences of Henry with whores prior to his relation with Catherine. But, now Jordon feels that the ecstasy he has derived from his sexual encounter with Maria is no ordinary thing. When he reaches orgasm, he feels:

> ...it was a dark passage which leads to nowhere, then to nowhere, then again to nowhere, once again to nowhere, always and forever to nowhere, heavy on the elbows in the earth to nowhere, dark, never any end to nowhere, now not to be borne once again always and to nowhere, now beyond all bearing up, up, up and into nowhere, scaldingly holdingly, all nowhere gone and time absolutely still and they were both there, time having stopped and he felt the earth move out and away from under them![84]

The manifold repetitions of the word 'nowhere' give a suggestion of a stage of feeling in which the conscious ceases to operate. It is a mystic experience which every spiritual adept gathers at the time of his communion with the divine. This state of consciousness of timelessness (time absolute still) with no vision of past and future is, in fact, a mystical experience of 'Love' in the course of sexual relationship. From now onwards, Jordan regards Maria, not as a girl, but as a 'wife'. He starts weaving a rosy dream of a future which he may celebrate with her after the successful execution of the mission. Like Henry and Catherine, Jordan and Maria think that, they are one soul in two bodies. When Jordan is lying with Maria, he speaks:

> 'Can you not feel my heart be your heart?'
>
> 'Yes, there is no difference.'
>
> 'Now, feel. I am thee and thou art me and all of one is the other. And I love thee. Oh, I love thee so. Are we not truly one? Canst thou not feel it?'
>
> 'Yes he said, 'It is true.'[85]

Now, Jordon and Maria have become one. Thus, 'Love' is no ordinary physical relationship. Both Jordan and Maria feel much confidence in facing the constant danger of life. 'Love' does not restrain him from doing his duty. It makes Jordan see the realities of life on his pulse, and the confidence to face them enhances. Therefore, Jordan comes to understand that life is not a daily round of eating, drinking and making merry. There is something more in life than we can think of. He sees a life in which one can do something for someone else also. No longer does he see life from his own point of view but from that of Maria. He weaves a world homeliness and domesticity in which Maria is the centre of attraction. He has gathered a new awareness to for someone else, to create happiness for others and, to die for some other persons. Thus, the vision of his life is widened and enlarged.

> Do you know that until I met thee I have never asked for anything? Nor wanted of anything except the movement and the winning of this war. Truly I have been very pure in my ambition I have worked much and now I love thee, he said it now in a complete embracing of all that would not be, I have thee, I love all that we have fought for. I love thee as I love liberty and dignity and the rights of all men to work and not be hungry. I love thee as love Madrid that we have defended and as I love all my comrades that have died and may have died. Many. Many. Thou cannot think now many. But, I love thee as love what I love most in the world and I love thee more. I love thee very much rabbit. More than I can tell thee. But I say this now to tell thee a little. I have never had a wife and now I have thee for a wife and I am happy.[86]

This is a new realization of 'self'. Jordon's 'self' till now has been partly realized in the horrors and dangers of war but now it gets fulfilled in the new and stark love born out of the happy physical union with Maria. This sort of love does not enfeeble his power to act promptly. Hemingway's vision of sex and love is that they are a great prompting force on the path of duty. Jordan gets over-confident in tackling his arduous task of blowing-up the bridge. He knows well that the death is almost a sure fate in the execution of this plan, but he feels emboldened enough to face it.

He felt the long light body, warm against him, comforting against him, abolishing loveliness against him, magically by a simple touching of flanks; of soldiers and of feet, making an alliance against death with him.[87]

Now, Jordan is ready to face death more confidently. When he gets seriously injured while escaping with the men of Pablo, he asks them to leave him to die alone. But then, he tells Maria, a symbol of Love, which remains immortalized, though love perishes, love, exists:

> 'What I do now I do alone I could not do it well with thee. If thou goest then I go too. Do you not see how it is? Which over one there is, is both.'
>
> 'I will stay thee.'
>
> 'Nay, rabbit, Listen. That people cannot go together. Each one must do it alone. But if thou goes then I go with thou. It is in that way that I go too. Thou will go now, I know. For thou art good and go now, I know. For thou art good and kind them will go new for us both .... There is no good bye, gupp, because we are not apart.'[88]

Here, Jordan reveals one of the basic realities of life which Hemingway wants everyone to know –that one must suffer a loss, may it be of life or relation. But love born out of the physical relationship between a man and a woman provides stamina to face the consequences with the satisfaction that one has realized one's real self in the process of making a commitment beyond one's self. Though lovers die, yet love exists. Since, 'love' is no more a physical phenomenon; death of partners does not matter. In Farewell to Arms, Catherin, the beloved, dies and in For Whom the Bell Tolls the lover dies. Nevertheless, both Henry and Jordon are confidently active in facing reality because of the latent energy of love in their hearts. Their belief is that since both the lover and the beloved are 'one', 'love' will continue to exist on the earth even if one of the partners passes away. Thus it, is in love born out of sex that human beings realize their 'self' and get ready for action -this forms an indispensable awareness for the protagonists of Hemingway. Sex bereft of love is futile. It is the fusion of sex and love which makes life worth living.

4

An Encounter with Death: An Advocate of Action and Optimism

Before the Renaissance, God was the measure of all things. He was the kernel of creation, the still centre and the prime mover. People had faith in what the apostle of religion preached and dared not out step the bounds of religion. That is, the individuality of the people was submerged under the deadweight of customs and religions. A man existed because he believed. With the coming of Renaissance, the comfortable sensibility of the people received a jolt which awakened in them the awareness of awareness of individuality. What was suppressed in the Middle Ages in the West was a subject of glorification in Indian Metaphysics, particularly in the Yoga sutra of Patanjali. The Yoga sutra of Patanjali stresses the mystic truth that human body is the treasure of infinite potentiality which, if properly exploited, leads to the union with supreme consciousness or what Emerson calls 'Oversoul'. This consciousness, though in a very little degree, dawned upon the people of the Renaissance. The difference lies in the fact that while the exponents of Indian Metaphysics stress the need for bodily glorification for union with Brahma, the people of the Renaissance glorified the body for the sake of body. Bacon's opening line in his essay Of Studies makes it perfectly clear that studies aim at providing delight and ornament. Studies do not add to the spiritual enlightenment. Marlowe's protagonists are individuals -be he Doctor Faustus or the Jew of Malta, Tamberlaine or King Edward II. Each character does his best to break away from the bonds of established religion and create new values. The Jew of Malta in his lust for wealth or Doctor Faustus in his inordinate passion for knowledge is a atypical man of the Renaissance. Doctor Faustus who is compared with Icarus in his ambition sells his soul to the Devil and pursues knowledge. This shows the strong individuality of Doctor Faustus. Even the characters of Shakespeare are individualized -Macbeth in his ambition and intense imagination is the crowning glory of individuality.

All this shows that the advent of Renaissance opened up a new vista of optimism perceptible in the emphasis shifted from God-centered universe to man-centered universe. Put in a different phraseology, Man and not God is considered the centre of the universe and hence Man is considered to be all-powerful and all sufficient in himself. The glorification of man as is clear from Hamlet's words 'What a piece of work is man!' fostered the theory of individualism. The emphasis on self-abnegation glorified in the Middle Ages gave way to the assertion of self. This assertive self is the active self. Inertia is negative of the self. Therefore, to assert self is to activise it to perfection. Hemingway's saga of action is nothing but this struggle of soul to carve out its own existence undeterred by the obstacles and impediments in life. It is, therefore, but natural that 'self' should acquire a new significance. The self of man lies in being sufficient. The gradual decline in human relationship, the point of utmost consideration in the middle age, was fuelled by a quest of economic and social security. The modern world witnesses man as a lone figure who has to rely upon his own potentiality in shaping his destiny. This individualism resulted in the fragmentation of the ancient institutions like society and family. Naturally, a man asserting his individual 'self' becomes a lone figure. R.S.Thomas, in a poem entitled 'Here' rightly expresses the perplexity and bewilderment of man who is in a fix to decide where to go. He says:

> I have nowhere to go
> The swift satellites show
> The clock of my whole being is slow.[89]

Various European dramatists and novelists have depicted the tragic condition of an individual's fractured 'self', which is essentially estranged from human beings. Tennessee Williams, in his drama, A Street Car Named Desire, shows the female protagonist, Blanche, all alone in the world trying to build up her life in one way or the other. But, she experiences shattering blows. In a very pathetic tone, she says: "I have been going from one leaky roof to another leaky roof."[90] A solitary individual fails to realize his 'self'. Robert Penn Warren, too, in At Heaven's Gate exhibits the tragic condition of a lone individual woman trying to live life on her own terms. In celebrating the life, she shifts her affection from one lover to another only to end in utter disillusion. A degenerate lover who makes her pregnant and then refuses to marry kills her. The haunting ghost of loneliness and solitude ex-communicates the human 'self' to such an extent as the whole generation of the human beings feel life to be an awesome burden to be shouldered all alone. The optimism of Robert Frost which finds expression in the following lines:

> Woods are lovely dark and deep
> But I have promises to keep
> And miles to go before I sleep
> And miles to go before I sleep.[91]

The poet can no longer captivate the fancy of an

individual for the simple reason that every man has become an island to himself. Ernest Hemingway, along with his contemporaries John Steinbeck and Robert Penn Warren, has explored the growing menace of individualism.

In his novel The Sun Also Rises, he shows Brett, Cohn, Jake, Mike and others leading a life of vagabond. They roam from one club to another, one place to another, without any purpose. Cohn has divorced his first wife, and is going to marry another woman. But, as he sees Brett, he pursues her, and tries to enjoy her company at the cost of his prestige in society and relation with his friends. Brett is a whimsical woman. She always changes one man after another. She has divorced her first husband and is engaged to Mike. But, she enjoys Cohn's company and money too. He is a wealthy count who remains her bosom friend. In Spain, she develops love for Romero. Whenever she receives any setback in love, she is confident of being helped by Jake. Jake has become impotent in an accident during war. He is a wastrel. His main occupation of life is to go from one club to another, squander money on wine and women for temporary relief, and observe the activities of Brett with pain. Mike is a sentimental fool who is shocked at the flippant behavior of Brett, and drinks wine beyond his monetary strength. Thus, all the people are asserting their individualities. But to what end? Hemingway points out that individualism to an extreme extent leads to a disorganization of life and loss of self. These individuals are living in crowds or company. But their self is solitary and isolated. Matthew Arnold had pertinently observed about Modern individuals:

> Yes! in the sea of life enisled
> With echoing straits between us thrown
> Dotting the shoreless watery wild
> We mortal millions live alone.[92]

In his next novel To Have and Have Not, Hemingway breaks fresh ground by introducing a new element about the concept of man's solitary 'self' amidst a sea of pain and suffering. This new element is the discovery or, perhaps, the realization of the significance of constancy and loyalty in human relationship, in short, of the value of solidarity. The protagonist of the novel, Harry Morgan, suffers much at the hands of a force beyond his control. He suffers economic crisis due to the treachery of one of the passengers on board the ship. This passenger welshes on payment for lost fishing tackle. Morgan becomes bankrupt and is coerced into activities –illegal and anti-social. He agrees to smuggle the Chinese from Cuba into the U.S.A. Apprehending danger, he cunningly manages to kill their leader and take money and leave others. While smuggling illegal liquor, he is entrapped in a gun battle with federal officers. He fights with them with utmost courage and valour. But, as ill-luck would have it, he loses an arm. Besides, his boat is confiscated. The financial crisis which catches him unawares shakes him to the morrow. Overcoming the momentary phase of crisis with undaunted courage, he chalks out a plan to steal a boast and smuggles Cubans into the U.S.A. Unfortunately, he meets four gangsters who have committed robbery in a bank. He is ordered to take them to the U.S.A. He sails towards the destination. But, he fears that the robbers will kill him as they reach their destination. Partly to get their money and partly to save his own life, he takes a grave risk of killing the four men. He achieves his mission, but during the operation, he himself receives a bullet injury in his abdomen. He is fully conscious of the fact that his family will have to suffer untold sufferings from economic crisis and there is no way out to help them. Up till now, Harry Morgan was fighting with the odds of life and alone – single-handed with zeal and courage. Hemingway gives a very touching description of a loan modern man sacrificed at the altar of unavoidable circumstances.

> Harry Morgan lay there on the iron pipe bank. His eyes were closed but he opened them when the

> captain touched his wide shoulder. "How you feeling, Harry?" the captain asked him Harry Morgan looked at him and did not speak. Can we get anything, boy?[93]

Morgan, at the point of death, is willing to communicate his realization of life. A lone individual's pathetic condition has been revealed. The question comes forward where does the self of Morgan exists? The unbridled and devastating forces of society in which no one lends a helping hand have annihilated his self. It reminds us of Dos Passos's Adventures of A young Man in which Glenn Spotswood, the protagonist, leads a revolutionary life. He helps to organize labour unions especially in some mining districts of Pennsylvania and undergoes all the hardships and injustices of the company pressure. But, he realizes that the party is more interested in its own success than the fate of an individual workers. He leaves America to join the International Brigades in the Spanish Civil War, is suspected of being a Trotskyite, gets arrested and is killed in a skirmish. Here, Doss Passos is reinforcing the idea, highlighted by Hemingway that the self of an individual has lost its dignity in the present socio-economic order.

Morgan has been trying to build up his life with individual effort. His self has been all-alone through the myriad adventures of life. Though, he never accepts defeat, yet, at the point of death, he realizes that a lone individual cannot assert his 'self'. Hemingway gives a very scintillating account of Harry Morgan's manner of communicating the real crux of life:

> 'Who did it, Harry?' the mat asked.
>
> 'Harry looked at him.'
>
> 'Don't fool yourself'; he said. The captain and the mate both bent over him. Now it was coming.
>
> 'Like trying to pass cars on the top of hills. On that road in Cuba. On any road. Anywhere. Just

> like that. I mean how things are. The way that they been going. For a while yes sure all-right. May be with luck. A man'. He stopped. The captain shook his head at the mate again. Harry Morgan looked at him flatly. The captain wet Harry's lips again. They made a bloody mark on the towel.
>
> 'A man' Harry Morgan said, looking at them both.
>
> 'One man alone ain't got. No man alone now.' He stopped. No matter how a man alone ain't got no bloody chance.'
>
> 'He shut his eyes. It had taken him a long time to get it out and it had taken him all of his life to learn it. He laid there his eyes open again. 'Come on', said the captain to the mate.
>
> 'You sure you' don't want anything. Harry?'
>
> 'Harry Morgan looked at him but he did not answer.' He had told them, but they had not heard.[94]

This is a commentary on extreme individualism that Hemingway has so far experienced. He suggests that the socio-economic order of the world does not permit the blossoming of 'self' of the human being, it must be achieved through collective action, for a solitary man has no chance whatsoever to realize his 'self'. This has been vivified in the subsequent novel, For Whom the Bell Tolls.

In For Whom the Bell Tolls, Hemingway shows a definite development in his vision of an individual's predicament in the world. He comes to believe that a man needs solidarity of other in the adventure through the ordeal of life and that a man can also live a life by his own 'self'. He discounts the insignificance and pessimism attached to an individual in life. Jordon, the protagonist, is on a mission to blow a bridge in an Italian occupied Spanish territory. Jordon meets a band of Guerrillas who inhabit a nearby mountain. He develops a unique type of affection for the Guerrillas. Agustin, Pilar, Anselmo,

Fernando, Maria and others develop a very close and touching relation with one another. When Romero goes to another hill spot to meet El Sordo, he develops a heart-felt relation with Joaquin and El Sordo. Pilar reveals her past, how she was married to Finito, a bull-fighter, and how after his death, she got engaged with Pablo. Here, the narration of the brutal murders in course of the movement against Italy's fascism and her feelings thereof become part and parcel of Romero's own experiences of life. Pilar is ready to go to any extent to help Jordan in executing his mission. Thus, a very strong bond of relationship exists between the two. It helps in diminishing the feeling of loneliness, and gives encouragement to Jordon. Maria's revelation of the past, when she led a peaceful life with her father, mother, brothers and sisters, and the subsequent annihilation of the members of her family by the fascists, brings Jordon very close to her. She had been raped by the fascists for so a long time and beaten so brutally that Jordon could not help loving intensely. Maria says:

> But I know not how. Where things were done to me I fought until I could not see. I fought until-until-until one sat upon my head -and I bit him -and then they tried my mouth and help -my arms behind my head and others did things to me.
>
> 'I love thee, Maria', he said 'And no one has done anything to thee. Thee, they cannot touch. No one has touched thee, little rabbit.'
>
> 'You believe that?'
>
> 'I know it.'
>
> 'And you can love me?' Warm again against him now.
>
> 'I can love thee more.'[95]

Jordan's admiration for Maria is so strong that he becomes restless to assuage her in injured feelings. It is by virtue of his intense love that Maria regains her identity. But, unlike Henry's relation with Catherine in A Farewell to Arms, Jordan's relation with Maria prompts him to execute his duty with accuracy and confidence. Henry escapes from army to live with Catherine. But, Jordan's love for Maria actuates him to participate in war with vigour and zeal.

Jordan develops a very profound relation with Anselmo. The destruction of the family of Anselmo and his tragic experiences of life are very spontaneously responded by Jordan. Anselmo feels a natural hatred against killing human beings. Jordan, too, experiences the same. But, both are ready to indulge in brutal massacre, if duty makes it indispensable. Their close relation is shown in the conversation:

> 'Listen' he said to Anselmo. 'I'm awfully glad to see you.'
>
> 'And me to see thee', the old man said.
>
> 'As they went up the hill in the dark, the wind at their backs, the storm blowing past them as they climbed, Anselmo did not feel lonely. He had not been lonely since Ingles had clapped him on the shoulder. The Ingles was pleased and happy and they joked together. The Ingles said it all went well and he was not worried. The drink in his stomach warmed him and his feet were warming, now climbing.
>
> 'Not much on the road', he said to the Ingles.
>
> 'Good', the Ingles told him. 'You will show me when we get there.'
>
> Anselmo was happy now and he was very pleased that he had stayed there at the post of observation.[96]

This unique relationship between the two is important for the accomplishment of the mission of blowing the bridge.

His relation with El Sordo is no less strong as is evident from their conversation:

> 'I appreciate your aid and your loyalty', Robert Jordan said. 'I appreciate the difficulty caused by the timing of the blowing of the bridge.'
>
> 'Don't talk of that' El Sordo said, 'We are here to do what we can do.'[97]

It is this feeling of mutual admiration and love that makes El Sordo sacrifice his life with confidence.

Hemingway reaches the climax of his artistic faculty when he shows how spontaneously each person is ready to share the misery and pain with the other and explores avenues to the same. Pilar, Maria and Jordan are spontaneously drawn towards Joaquin, when he reveals his quandary. His father, mother and sister have been slain or shot down by the fascists. He feels utterly helpless and hopeless. The feeling of isolation taxes his mind so much that he cannot help breaking down before Jordan, Pilar and Maria while relating his misfortune.

> As the boy stood there, Maria reached up, puts her arms around his neck and kissed him. Joaquin turned his head away because he was crying. 'That is as a brother', Maria said to him.
>
> 'I kiss thee as a brother.'
>
> The boy shook his head, crying without making any noise.
>
> 'I am thy sister.' Maria said. 'And I love thee and thou hast a family we are all thy family.'[98]

Thus, a family-feeling develops among them, and it is a great help to Joaquin in reasserting his 'self'. It is this feeling of family-relation that makes the mission of bridge blowing significant. Thus, this family feeling strengthens the self of Joaquin.

Pablo feels dissatisfied with Jordan and frankly

expresses his disapproval of the mission. At the night of the day on which the bridge is to be blown up, Pablo steals away important detonators. Jordan and his friends feel much humiliated at this unexpected occurrence. But, Pablo feels alienated, once he runs away from his friends, and is constrained to retreat with men and horses required for blowing the bridge.

> He looked at Robert now.
>
> 'When I left I thought you would know that it was impossible and would give it up. Then after I had thrown away thy material I saw it is another manner.'
>
> 'I am glad to see thee'. Robert Jordan said. He walked over to me. 'We are all right with the grenades. That will work. The other does not matter now.'
>
> 'Now', Pablo said, 'I do nothing for thee. Thou art a thing of bad omen. All of this comes from thee. Sordo also. But after I had thrown away thy material I found myself too lonely.[99]

It is this feeling of solidarity that makes them blow the bridge successfully. This has also been emphasized by Steinbeck. In Grapes of Wrath, he emphasizes the virtues of solidarity of individuals for the realization and amelioration of 'self'. The family of Ma Joad undergoes severe economic pressure. But, the unity and close relation with one another dispels its poignant effect. Ma Joad tries tooth and nail to keep this unity intact, for his individual self gets annihilated in facing the miseries of life alone.

Hemingway is not a vain idealist. He knows that solidarity among human beings is necessary, but it is only a temporal measure to assuage the discontent and pain of an individual. Jordan sustains a fracture in a thighbone while escaping with guerillas. Now, he has to decide whether he should be there to ensure the sage-retreat of his companions or go with them and endanger the security of the entire party. Jordan has intense love for Maria. She has become a symbol of Spain, freedom, love and ideal womanhood for Jordan. In spite of Maria's pressure of entreaties, Jordan declines to go with the guerillas because he has not only lived his full life, but also there lies in his stay the safety of the group. Even he is on the point of death, he escapes from the temptation of committing suicide by thinking about them;

> Think about them being away, he said. Think about them crossing a creek. Think about them riding through the heather. Think about them going up the slope. Think about them ok to night. Think about them travelling all night. Think about them hiding up tomorrow. Think about them. That's just as far I can think about them, he said.[100]

Jordan passes away from this world with the satisfaction that his friends have gone away with security. Hemingway shows the virtue of solidarity. But, then, he also emphasizes the importance of individual. It becomes as clear as day light that large aims are indispensable dependent upon smaller aims and that the over-all victory over Segovia is dependent on individual aims. The importance is demonstrated by the conflict raging in the mind of the protagonist. He comes alone and he passes away from this world all alone. The solidarity among individuals is a temporal measure to console one's self. Hemingway, the realist, knows this fact and it has been elaborately dealt with in his last novel The Old Man and the Sea.

In The Old Man and the Sea, Hemingway has presented an epic struggle of a lone fisherman in the sea of difficulties, and tragedies of human life. The old man has not been able to catch any fish for the last eighty-four days. Everyone thinks him to be an unlucky and retired fisherman who is good-for-nothing. The boy who used to go with the old man—Santiago is now forbidden by his parents to accompany him. The old man has a natural affection for the boy and the boy responds warmly. But, the old man, willingly compromises with his fate:

> 'I remember' the old man said. 'I know you did not leave me because you doubted.'
>
> 'It was Papa made me leave, I am a boy and I must obey him.'
>
> 'I know' the old man said. 'It is quite normal.'[101]

But, unlike the romantics who want to dilute the pain of loneliness with the magic of past, Santiago lives a life in the present:

> Once there had been a tinted photograph of his wife on the wall but he had taken it down because it made him too lonely to see it and it was on the shelf in the corner under his clear shirt.[102]

But, the old man is never in a complaining mood. Hemingway is pinpointing the strength and confidence with the modern man will have to face the ravages of the world. There is no use of bewailing on pathetic conditions of life or creating illusions. The old man, too, nurses a very optimistic idea that eighty-five is a lucky number. He talks about 'yellow rice' fish, and cast net, though "there was no cast net .... But they went through this fiction every day. There was no pot of yellow rice and fish and the boy knew this to."[103] But this illusion has been deliberately created to make humorous atmosphere. The old man does not take these humorous remarks to be facts of life. In Arthur Miller's The Death of a Salesman, the self-willed hopes and illusions of the merchant, become part and parcel of his life. By profession "riding on smile and shoeshine",[104] he realizes, in a number of visions of his earlier life, how he has not only over rated the talent of his elder son, but also misjudged his character, how the value of being well-liked is not necessarily a safe one, and how his big words have only laid to a disastrous result. But the old man (Santiago) does not make his optimism retard his dynamism; it only strengthens him to face the realities of life boldly.

The young boy helps the old man in sundry ways. He brings him food and baits of fishing and cast net, and does other things. The company of the boy is a great consolation for the old man. But, as he starts on the voyage of practical life (sea), there is no one to extend a helping hand. That is, the old man has to go through the world of action all alone. When he sets out early in the morning for fishing, he is alone. This 'sea' is a symbol of the vast and unending chain of difficulties of life and the fish is the definite goal, which the old man struggles to achieve. A man has to go through this sea to catch fish alone and solitary. Even in the loneliness, this old man does not feel depressed. All the time he is conscious of playing the game of fish catching in the most effective way. There is no one to talk to him; no one to refresh his memory; no one to allay his grief at his failure to catch fish; and no one to praise his dynamism. Hemingway's old man is alone but strong enough to brave the world alone. The old man can be constrasted with Gatsby, the protagonist of The Great Gatsby. Gatsby feels utterly dissatisfied living alienated from the society and, therefore, arranges big parties to have company and social relation. He tries hard to get back to his beloved who is now married to another man. This shows the intense obsession of the protagonist with his alienated 'self'. But, Hemingway's Santiago does not show any such weakness. He shows remarkable stamina in facing the ravages of the world quite alone.

If there is no one to converse with him in the sea, he consoles himself by taking to birds, fishes and winds. When a big fish, which has been caught, is deep down in the sea, Santiago is pained for sitting so long with no movement. He starts talking with a bird that comes, forwards the stiff from the north and flies very low over the water:

> The bird made the stern of the boat and rested

there. Then he flew around the old man's head and rested on the line where he was more comfortable.

'How old are you? the old man asked the bird.

'Is this your first trip?'

The bird looked at him when he spoke. He was too tired even to examine the line and he teetered on it as his delicate fact gripped it fast.

'It's steady,' the old man told him. 'It's too steady. You shouldn't be that tired after a windless night. What are birds coming to?'

The hawks, he thought, that come out to sea to meet them. But he said nothing of this to the bird who could not understand him anyway and who would learn about the hawks soon enough.

'Take a good rest, small bird,' he said. 'Then go in and take your chance like any man or bird or fish'.

It encouraged him to talk because his back had stiffened in the night and it hurt truly now.

'Stay at my house if you like, bird,' he said. 'I am sorry I cannot hoist the sail and take you in with the small breeze that is rising. But I am with a friend.'[105]

He talks with the fish, wind, water and sun to the feeling of boredom. In fact, he talks with himself, for there is no one with whom he can have any recommendation. But, the condition of the old man is different from that of Prufrock who indulges in self-talking to exhibit his fractured and dormant self.

Let us go then, you and I,
When evening is spread out against the sky
Like a patient etherised upon a table;[106]

Here 'you' and 'I' suggest the bifurcation of the self of Prufrock. The expression "a patient etherised upon a table" suggests the passive and dormant self of the protagonist who is unable to indulge in any way creative and active actions. But, Santiago's self-talk is a source of confidence. It is, no doubt, a compulsion but it is also a pleasure for Santiago. It generates a new energy in his body and mind to encounter the ravages of Nature. Hence, Hemingway makes 'self-talk' a source of consolation and regeneration for isolated individual, instead of dejection and despair. Prufrock appears to have lost his self in his self-talk. But Santingo appears to asserting his self in the process.

When Santiago is in the process of killing the fish, he has to face many hardships. Quite often, he is reminded of the young boy who would have rendered incalculable service:

> If the boy was here he would wet the coils of line, he thought. Yes. If the boy were here. If the boy were here.[107]

The fact is, the boy is not there and will never be there, and that Santiago will have to carry out the operation, catch the fish alone and quite alone. He undergoes terrible pain. A violent scuffle ensues between the big fish and that old man. The latter exercises all tricks and maneuverings to kill the fish. At times, it does appear that the old man is going to lose the game as one has seen in the tussle between Moby Dick and Captain Ahab in Herman Melville's Moby Dick. The captain in Moby Dick has many men to back him. Here, Santiago has none. He is all alone. In this hair-raising struggle, there is no one to give him even a little help. But, the old man Santiago with full dignity goes on with his work. He says:

> 'But man is not made for defeat', he said. 'A man can be destroyed but not defeated.[108]

It is this dictum of life which impels him to continue

his struggle till he achieves his victory. The old man ties the fish with the posterior part of the ship and starts sailing towards the shore of his habitation, though he has no compass to guide him. Hemingway knows well that no individual can get any permanent victory or gain. It is merely an ideal. When the old man is returning with his fish, sharks pounce upon the flesh of the fish. The old man once again renew his zeal to put a tough fight against the sharks. In the process, he loses his harpoon, breaks his knife and injures his hands. At last, he fails to prevent the sharks from devouring the marlin. When he reaches the shore, his marlin is but a mere skeleton. The lone man has been defeated in this problematic world. Hemingway asserts that the self of an individual has to exist alone and estranged from all, as the old man was in the sea, and that the aim of life for which one will have to try tooth and nail is not likely to be accomplished. But, the self of man lies not in being depressed but facing reality. Man has come alone and will go alone from this world. Therefore, loneliness and alienation are the crux of life that one will have to accept as real. Naturally, depression and disappointment will not pay any good. At the end of The Old Man and the Sea, Hemingway writes:

> Up the road, in his shack, the old man was sleeping again. He was still sleeping on his face and the boy was sitting by him watching him. The old man was dreaming about the lions.[109]

The dream of the lion is suggestive of the assertion of the old man's fight with the forces of Nature. Therefore, it may be noted that Hemingway emphasizes that an individual has to keep faith in his own self, for group or society can, at least, provide only momentary relief:

> Brought to life in the middle of the Great Depression, Harry Morgan in To Have and Have Not may mumble at his death, 'a man alone ain't go no bloody chance', but Jake Barnes, Frederick Henry, Robert Jordan, and Santiago give the world

> another message: Anything a man does, anything a man really does, he does from courage of his own breast. There is no help –no cavalry over the hill, no god in the machine, no salvation in membership.[110]

Thus, it is in accepting the predicament of a lone man and in struggling against it that real 'self' of man is manifested.

The way Hemingway stresses the individuality of his characters reminds us of Hardy's characters who struggle and never yield. For example, we can take The Return of the Native. Clym Yeobright, the protagonist of this novel, has to encounter hurdles and obstacles at every step. When he returns to Egdon Health with a view to improving the condition of the people by spreading education, he is struck with practical blindness. It seems that all his hopes and aspirations have been blighted. He seems to stagger under the fatal blows of a series of bad luck. But, he is not an anemic character who can stoop to what the President of Immortals has destined for him. In order to destroy the sense of depression, he takes to furze cutting which inspires him with a new hope and zeal. A weak-willed character would have yielded to such adverse circumstances of life. Clym Yeobright knows well how to tilt the balance of what is determined to his favour and pulls himself out of depression and dejection. It is his unyielding nature that reveals a personality which cannot but grow even in the midst of the odds of life. What is true of Clym Yeobright in The Return of The Native is also true of Henchard, the protagonist of The Mayor of the Casterbridge. He dies but heroically. Naturally, the tragic death which is brought about by his inordinate passion does not generate a sense of pathos. We see the glory of an individual even when he is crushed under the weight of miseries. Gabriel Oak, the protagonist of Far From the Madding crowd, though not a tragic character, is a powerful individual. Like the protagonist of The Old Man And The Sea, he has to experience a number of mishaps. He loses his sheep. The worst of all is that he fails to win the affection of Bathsheba. Still, he struggles, and it is towards the end of the novel that he is amply rewarded for his patient sufferings. The old man succeeds in catching the fish after eighty-four days. Likewise, Gabriel Oak succeeds in winning the affection of Bathsheba after a patient suffering of months. Thus, the characters neither of Hardy nor of Hemingway yield to the blows of fate or adverse circumstances. What does all this show? Individuality. Each character of Hemingway is individual enough to fight to the last to achieve the mission of his life. Hemingway's characters come very close to those of Joyce Cary. Cary's characters, like those of Hemingway, are unyielding. In his novel Mister Jonson, the novelist presents the protagonist who has a strong individuality. It is, therefore, but natural that he should not be swayed by customs and tradition. Everywhere does he try to assert his individuality. The way he asserts his individuality is not very different from that of Jordan who, in a bid to make his life worth living, does all that society disapproves but individuality approves.

Death has been a subject matter of discussion -literary as well as metaphysical. If Shakespeare and Shirley perceive in death a leveling power, John Donne in his poem "Death Be Not Proud" presents death as something impotent, for death cannot harm the soul. So, what is an object of fear for the common people does not chill the men of letters with a sense of pessimism. Poets, with a mystic awareness of life, see no distinction between life and death. "Death and Life", a poem by Sri Aurobindo, suggests the mystical truth that there is nothing like death; it is life in disguise. Modern poets, playwrights and novelists deal as much with the nature of death as with the fear of death. Harold Pinter, in many of his plays, has expressed his obsession with death through his characters. In his play Birthday Party, he demonstrates that the fear of death is oppressing the soul of Stanley, a symbol of modern man. Two strangers

-Goldberg and MacCann -are the merchants of death. They want to oust him from his room -a symbol of his secured and independent self. But, at last, he succumbs to their pressure. Hardy's characters have something which is commonly designated as fear complex and as such adverse circumstances of life strikes such a terror into their hearts that they firmly believe that 'Happiness is the occasional episode in a general drama of pain.' The poets and playwrights of the past depict the fear so dramatically and vividly that the reader cannot but feel that death is something which must be faced dauntlessly. The courage to face death has been exemplified in most of the ancient works of art. Knights in the Middle Ages set out on the path of adventures to release their beloveds from the clutches of demons and giants. Malory's prose work Morte D'Arthur is an illustration of this truth. Even Spenser's The Faerie Queen concretely visualizes the march of Red Cross Knight through trials and tribulations, toils and temptations, so that he may protect those who are in peril. His onward march in the teeth of dangers and difficulties reflects the vigour of his individuality to stare in the face of death. Shakespeare's Macbeth, when he is killed, is not reduced to pathetic helplessness, because he dies heroically. Similar is the case with the Duchess of Malfi, the protagonist of Webster. Before she dies, she says 'I am still the Duchess of Malfi'. In moments of death, she attains the tragic dignity which does not characterize the heroine of Middleton in The Changeling. Beatrice Joanne, the protagonist of The Changeling is so much overcome with a sense of grief and remorse that she says: 'It is better to die when it is shame to live.'[111] What the people faced boldly and smilingly in the past has affected modern people adversely. People are so much gripped with a sense of fear that they are incapacitated enough to do anything. That this fear prevents people from doing something has been presented in Eliot's poem The Love Song of J. Alfred Prufrock where Prufrock who lacks courage to propose to his beloved, only dreams of being in the grip of death (the Eternal Footman):

I am no prophet -and here's no great matter;

I have seen the moment of my greatness flicker,

And I have seen the eternal Footman hold my coat, and

snicker,

And in short, I was afraid.[112]

"Death", the fear of death, has become an obsession with the modern man. The demon of barbarity let loose by the first and second world wars has staged a death's dance reducing all human values to a heap of broken images. A skylark soaring in the sky activated the imagination of Shelley:

Teach me half the gladness

That thy brain must know,[113]

Disturbed modern people take the skylark for a symbol of death, because of its likeness with an enemy war -plane out to wipe their existence. In Measure for Measure, when Claudio is sentenced to death, the Duke exhorts him to accept death with humility for

Thou hast nor youth nor age;

But, as it were, an after-dinner's sleep,

Dreaming of both;[114]

But Claudio in Shakespeare's play Measure for Measure takes a romantic view of Death and says:

I will encounter darkness as a bride,

And hug it in mine arms.[115]

Similarly, Antony in Shakespeare's play Antony and Cleopatra happily utters:

but I will be

A bridegroom in my death, and run into't

As to a lover's bed,[116]

This romantic vision of accepting death as an inevitable phenomenon of life has been shattered by the modern incidents. The menace of 'death' came not only from war but also from the bloody events of daily life. This fear of death has had severe repercussions on the 'self' of man. This feeling has obsessed the modern men to such an extent that they have been reduced to 'selfless being' living under the constant shadow of death. The fake chivalric attitude towards death has become the target of mockery. In Arms And The Man the chivalric attitude exhibited by Major Serjius in facing death in war has been ridiculed by George Bernard Shaw. Tolstoy, in War and Peace, shows how Dragon-shaped fear of death impinges upon the very 'self' of man who cannot imagine a life of peace and happiness. This fear of death is an important feature in modern literature. It is this fear complex of death that makes W. H. Auden exclaim:

> The mass and majesty of this world, all
>
> That carries weight and always weighs the same
>
> Lay in the hands of others; they were small
>
> And could not hope for help and no help came
>
> What their foes liked to do was done, their shame
>
> Was all the worst could wish; they lost their pride
>
> And dies as men before their bodies died.[117]

People have become so much obsessed with death under this constant danger that Schopenhauer, the German philosopher, has said at a place; if one asks crops lying in a grave to come and live in the world, he will reject the offer, for the life in grave is better than the life in the world.[118] It is in this worldwide depression of the self of man, when it has lost the power of its assertion that Ernest Hemingway comes before the modern world with a vision of life which is equal with that of Nietzsche. Nietzsche, another German philosopher, proclaimed: 'God is dead'.[119] Naturally, the modern man appears bereft of all values. Nietzsche feels actually the predicament of modern man anchored to no definite goal. He explored many ways to encounter death, not to overcome it as the sages did in the past. It is possible to assert and realize the real in the past. Is it possible to assert and realize the real 'self' under such crippling fear of death? Nietzsche is the first realist who asserts that the 'self' of man can be realized not by escaping or running away from death but by facing it. Like a fearless tiger, he encourages the modern man to build their city near Venezola. Venezola is a volcano which erupts frequently taking the toll of many lives. But, this philosopher believes that the real thrill of life and the real 'self' of man lies in living by the side of this volcano and not in escaping away from it. Life lies in the thrill experienced by living in the midst of dangers. Eliot in his poetic drama, The Family Reunion, points out that salvation lies not in having an escape from death but in encountering it boldly. So long as Harry, the protagonist of the play, flies from the furies which haunt him everywhere, he is restless. He becomes so much restless that, at last, he stirs abroad to encounter it boldly. This is what Ernest Hemingway demonstrates through his novels. He has opened a new vision of optimism by actuating people to face the fear of death with confidence and love. While explaining the mentality of the people of Castella in Death in Afternoon, Hemingway writes:

> They know death is the unescapable reality, the one thing any man may be sure of; the only security; that it transcends all comforts and that with it you do not need a bath tub in every American home, nor, when you ... need the radio. They think a great deal about death and when they have a religion they have one which believe that life is much shorter than death. [120]

The novelist's primary concern is to emphasize the beauty and dignity of life while living in constant danger.

Living in a dream world or nursing illusions to escape from mortality is an object of ridicule or satire. Therefore, a hair-raising bull-fight becomes a universal symbol of true life for Hemingway. As a matador goes near a ferocious bull risking his life, it

> "takes a man out of himself and makes him feel immortal while it is proceeding, that gives him an ecstasy, that is, while momentary, as profound as any religious ecstasy; moving all the people in the ring together and increasing emotional intensity as it proceeds, carrying bull-fighter with it, he playing on the crowd through the bull and being moved as it responds in a growing ecstasy of ordered, formal, passionate, increasing disregard for death … ."[121]

In fact, there can be no happy end to love because in one way or the other life must break -either by death or by loss of affection, separation or physical degeneration. There are uncountable ways which lead to the loss of love and no man can build a fortress which can keep the destructive forces off. Then, the fact remains why one should fear death? The real self of man lies in accepting the inevitability of death. In The Sun Also Rises a very gloomy atmosphere has been created by Hemingway. A group of young men and women unmindful of the norms of life are seen in the pursuit of wine and women. Lady Ashley Brett, at times, has a clandestine affair now with Robert Cohn and now with her prospective husband, Mike. The protagonist of the novel, Jake who has become impotent because of an injury received during war, moves from one club to another trying to pass off time. He is also wildly in love with Brett. These expatriates living a life of ruffians do not understand the real meaning of life. In the novel Bill Gotten satirizes the wastrel kind of expatriates –

> You are an expatriate. You have lost touch with the soul. You get precious. Take, European scandals

> have ruined you. You drink yourself to death. You become obsessed by sex. You spend all your time talking or working. You are an expatriate, see? You hang around cafes?[122]

Hemingway is satirical towards these characters, who are ignorant of their real self. Naturally, he transports these characters to Spain to witness the dazzle of Fiesta. This game of Fiesta or Bull-fighting adds a new dimension to the novel. The bull-fighting is a game which is, in fact, a death game. A bull-fighter gets ready with his weapon to kill a bull, most ferocious and violent. Now, the bull-fighter has to kill the bull but it should be killed in a manner that gives maximum chance to the bull to kill the bull-fighter. Hemingway depicts bull-fight as a microcosmic tragedy. The death of the bull is inevitable but it must be caused by the observance of a ritual which gives the animal a free-chance to destroy the bull-fighter. Hemingway is attracted to this particular game because of its masculinity, its violence and its grave risk. Life is not a bed of roses and death is the reality of life, and the real existence of 'self' of man is possible in living in the neighborhood of the sincerest friend of life-death. In this bull-fighting, death and life shake hands with each other and the people, looking at the game clap in joy. The more energetically one risks one's life, the louder the clapping one gets from the people. This is the reality of life. Romero is the best bullfighter, for he infuriates the bull very virulently and then allows him to come so near him, so near, as if the bull were almost killing him. But, the play-boy, Romero skillfully saves himself and kills the bull. It is in this tension between life and death that the real 'self' of man exists. Jake comes to realize this fact. Naturally, he is shown taking no interest in the personal life of others and disengaging himself from everyone. At last, Brett calls him to rescue her from insolvency and then again, tries to avail herself of the weakness of Jakes. But she is shocked. This has been shown in the end of the novel. Jake and Brett are going in a taxi. Brett, resting comfortably against Jake, says: "O Jake, we would have had such a damned good time together."[123] Jake knows well that the life of which she is speaking is merely an illusion. He says pertinently, "Yes, Isn't it pretty to think so?"[124] The hidden irony of the statement is obvious. Thus, Hemingway by presenting the bull-fighting spectacle in which death is shown as an honest companion makes one realize the true essence of self.

In his next novel A Farewell to Arms, this fact has been explicitly demonstrated. The protagonist, Henry has a rosy dream about war. He spells out the chivalric picture of warfare. He is equally ignorant of the basics of love; for him, love with a woman is only a means of satisfying physical appetite. But, the breaking of war on Italian front and the subsequent injury shatters his rosy dream about war. He realizes after the injury by the mortar-shell that he is almost dead. He says:

> I went out swiftly, all of myself and I knew I was dead and it had all been a mistake to think that you just died. Then I floated and instead of going on, I felt myself slide back I breathe and I was back.[125]

In this way, Henry realizes that he is dead and has been so for a long time; and the mistake is in thinking that he has just died. The effect of the approaching death and the horror of the wound are sufficient enough to indoctrinate those values of life which the fear of death must inevitably destroy. When he is being admitted into the hospital of Milan, he realizes the purity of love - selfless love -by living with Catherine. They dream about a life which will promise them unmixed delight and love. Catherine becomes pregnant. But, they are not worried at all because they think that their life is an endless chain of joys. It is here that Hemingway is concerned with realities of life. Necessity, according to Hemingway, is born of life itself; it is inherent in human condition. Life must end in death and all commitment must end in loss.

But, this fact should not depress or distress one because one cannot escape inevitable realities of life, however hard one may try. Hemingway does his best to bring home this truth, by presenting the life of Henry and Catherine as an example. We are left into Catherine's ingrained fear of death. She is afraid of the rain because she sometimes feels:

> I am afraid of the rain because sometimes I see me dead in it.
>
> No,
>
> And sometimes I see you dead in it.[126]

In the novel, rain becomes a symbol of disaster. There is an indication that Henry is very little different from Catherine in his fear of death. They are in a café and it is raining.

> But at my back I always here
>
> Time's winged chariot hurrying near.[127]

He wants to talk facts as to where the baby will be born. Catherine refuses to discuss it. "Then don't worry darling."[128] She tells him, "You were fine until now and now you are worrying."[129] The tone of discussion suggests death; but at this stage, we do not know whose death it is to be. We see death face to face only at the end of the novel. Henry deserts the Italian army and meets her in Milan. But, the Italian police is always after Henry to arrest him. On a stormy night, a faithful waiter informs him of his arrest in the next morning. Catherine and Henry slip away on a boat to Switzerland. But, the change in place cannot change the course of death. Death shall follow no matter where he goes. The shadow of death starts taking a concrete shape on a violent rainy night. Catherine is admitted into a hospital, for she is in the last phase of pregnancy. Catherine's confinement is difficult and the delivery of the child is made possible through Caesarean operation. The specter of death of Catherine starts haunting Henry:

> Catherine has a good time in the time of pregnancy. It wasn't bad. She was hardly ever sick. She was not always uncomfortable until towards the last. So now they have got her in the end. You never got away with anything. Get away hail! It would have been the same if we had been married fifty times. And what if she should die? She won't die. People don't die in child's birth now a days. That was all husband's thought. Yes but what if she should die? She won't die .... But what if she should die. She can't die. Yes, but what if she should die? She can't, I tell you. Don't be a fool. It is just a bad time. It is just nature giving her hell .... Yes, but what if she should die? She can't die. Why would she die? What reason is there for her to die? There is just a child that has to be born the byproduct of the good nights at Milan. It makes trouble and is born and then you look after it and get fond of it may be. But what if she should die. She won't die. But what of she should die? She won't die. But what if she should die? Hey what about that?.... [130]

And this is what happens. The child is born dead. Catherine, too, is hovering between life and death. Henry fights tooth and nail to avert the blows of the inevitable death. He never believed in the existence of God and His mercy. But, he cannot help saying:

> I knew she was going to die and I prayed she would not. Don't let her die. Oh God please don't let her die. I will do anything for you if you don't let her die. I will do anything you say if you don't let her die. You took the baby. But, don't let her die. That was alright, but don't let her die.[131]

But, Hemingway is fully conscious of the fact that death, what Hardy calls 'Necessity', is indifferent to human appeal. Henry's hope that he would prevent her from dying is as illusory as his belief that he could escape war by singing a separate peace. His feeling is different from that of Longfellow who believes that death is not the end of life. The former believe that death is an end of life and the only value in death is man's knowledge of it. The centre of Hemingway's concept is that the game of life is logical, man-imposed, and man-created; the circumstances of life, mcre especially death are not. In the game of life, one is bound to lose and 'the harder you play, the more you lose'. The real essence of self of man lies in realizing and facing these facts.

In For Whom the Bell Tolls the fear of death has been concretely visualized. Jordan, an American, has been given the job of blowing a bridge in the area occupied by the fascists. Jordan knows that death in the execution of this mission is, more or less, certain. The fear of death does haunt him. But, this man knows well that death does not make life a puzzle rather, it provides an opportunity to him to realize the true 'self' of Man. His father had committed suicide. But Jordan is not only ready to compromise with death, when he meets the guerrillas living in a mountain cave near the bridge. The impression that Hemingway wants to create in the novel is that dangers to life are hanging all the way round. There can be no escape from it. The guerrilla's woman Pilar narrates the story of her first husband, Finito who was a brave bullfighter. He earned fame in killing bulls in the most risky manner. Pilar had asked him to give up this profession, for life is insecure on account of this. Once he is violently injured by the bull; but he gives very plausible explanation smiting to his wife:

> It is nothing, woman, Pilar, it is nothing. It should not have happened. I killed him very well. You understand. Nobody could have killed him better. Then having killed him exactly as I should and him absolutely dead, swaying on his legs, and ready to fall of his own weight, I walked away from him with a certain amount of amogance and much style and from the back he throws me. This horn between

> the cheeks of my buttocks and it comes out of my lever ... You and your safety did I live nine years with these of the worst paid matadors of the world not to learn about fear and about safety? [132]

This is how Hemingway presents his view of life. Further, when Pilar asks Jordon if he feels fear in the execution of this risky mission,

> And you have no fear
>
> ' 'Not' to die', he said truly.[133]

Jordan meets a very pathetic girl, Maria, who has lost the sense of herself in the frantic warfare of the fascist. She has been raped by so many people that no more realization of self is possible for her. A very delicate and emotional relation develops between Jordan and Maria. He even builds up a castle of imagination to go and live with Maria in Italy after the completion of his mission. The premonition of the death is always present in the novel. Nevertheless, not even the slightest touch of pessimism is allowed to dampen the zeal of Jordan. El Sordo, the leader of another band of guerrillas, is ready to help Jordan in accomplishing this task. Hemingway gives a very novel idea -what matters is present, life is always in present and the man's self exists in the assertion of present. El Sordo knows well that the kind of life they are living is bound to push them towards the jaws of death. But, it is not a matter of worry. 'If death will come, it will come, it is not present before me; therefore, no fear of death.' El Sordo knows well that to blow the bridge in the day time means death to all. But, he says:

> Listen to me, I am speaking much. It is so we any understand one another. We exist here by a miracle. By a miracle of laziness and stupidity of the fascists which they will remedy in time.[134]

Similarly, when the possibility of death is posed before Jordan, he says, "for me myself that is not important once the bridge is blown." At times, Jordan feels like abandoning his mission and living a happy life with Maria, for the death will depart him from his beloved forever. This feeling is only a temporary dilemma of Jordan.

> If this was how it was then this was how it was. But there was no law that made him say he liked it. I did not know that I could ever feel what I have felt, he thought. Nor that this could happen to me. I would like to have it for my whole life. You will, the other part of him said, you will. You have it now and that is your whole life is your whole life is; now, there is nothing else but now. There is neither the yesterday certainly, nor is there any tomorrow. How old must you be before you know that? There is only now, if now is only two days only days is your life and everything in it will be in proportion. This is how you live a life in two days. And if you stop complaining and asking for what you never will get, you will have a good life. A good life is not measured by any Biblical span.
>
> So now do not worry take what you have and do your work and you will have a long life and a very merry one. [135]

This is what Hemingway advocates -to live life in the present and that also, amidst dangers; there lies the real self of man.

The fascists trace Sordo and his men and there is every possibility of their death. Bullets fatally injure him. He knows that a few hours are more due to his life. He does not fear death but dying on a hill doesn't make him happy.

> He was not at all afraid of dying but he was angry at being trapped on the hill which was only utilizable as a place to die. If we could have gotten clear, he thought. If we could have come up the long valley or if we could have broken lose across the head, it would have been alright. But this

> chancre of a hill we must use it as well as we can and we have used it very well so fear.[136]

This is the stamina of Sordo. He knows that he is going to die. Still, he wants to kill some enemies before he dies. As a matter of fact, he kills two officers of the fascists. But, when the plane bombards from the air –

> All he could remember was at the hour of our death. Amen. At the hour of our death. Amen. At the hour. At the hour. Amen. The others all were firing. Not and at the hour of our death Amen.[137]

Thus they die a warrior's death.

Similarly, Hemingway shows that Jordan, too, is tense on the night before the day the mission is to be done. Though Jordan wavers, yet the force, what a psychologist would call, 'eros' gets the better of his spirit. Pablo throws away some of the grenades that were to be in blowing up the bridge and later comes back to confess his mistake –Jordan. In spite of this set-back, he struggles to make his mission a success, and he does succeed in achieving what he struggles for. When he is escaping on horse with Guerrillas, he receives a fatal injury in his leg; his thighbone gets dislocated. However, Pilar is ready to carry him on her horse, yet Jordan obstinately lies near a tree by the side of the curve of mountain. Maria does not want to leave him. But Jordan, a realist, knows that she will have to go from this place and that he will have to go from this world. After many requests, he persuades her to leave him alone to die. He says to her "Listen that people cannot do together. Each one must do it alone."[138] His loyal Guerrilla Agustin insists on remaining with him. Jordan orders him to go away. He says: "Go on, in war, there are many things like this."[139] When he is lying all alone with the pain over increasing and a machinegun in his hand, he feels like shooting himself. But, he is not the least hesitant in facing death. He believes that his life is short but worthy. What matters if life is short? He has enjoyed the life-span given to him. Death had to come, sooner or later. Death comes, but he is welcomed by Jordan. "and you had a lot of luck" he told himself,

> "to have had such to good life you have had just as good a life as grand fathers though not so long. You have had as good a life as any one because of these last days. You do not want to complain when you have been so lucky."[140]

As his pain is aggravated, the idea of suicide overpowers him. It is here that Hemingway shows that the heroism of a human being lies not in succumbing to death, but in fighting with it to the last. Even at this point, knowing well that death stares him in the face, he feels like killing a few soldiers before dying. The battle within his spirit is thought provoking to the very end. He is trying to ward off the blows of death before doing something positive. Therefore, firing with his machinegun, Jordan passes away from this world. It is not the death of Jordan that matters, but the way he faces death that makes him a heroic character and it is here that the real 'self' of man lies. His real self lies in transcending the fear of death and in going through the adventures of life and experiencing what Dylan Thomas says:

> And Death shall have no dominion
>
> Death man naked they shall be one
>
> With the man in the wind and the and the west moon
>
> Though they sink through the sea they shall rise again
>
> Though lovers be lost love shall not
>
> And death shall have no dominion.[141]

Hemingway's attitude towards life is different from that of Strindberg, Pirandello and Ionesco. These playwrights through their alienated protagonists project a pessimistic, nihilistic, or absurdist point of view.

Tennessee William's alienated protagonist, symbolizes unfulfilled and frustrated life which, however, can be repaired by letting sex work itself out smoothly and naturally O'Neill shows that if man is deified, he is reduced to the status of a mere thing. This is what Eugene O'Neill shows us happening to Yank in The Hairy Ape. Life becomes insupportable to him unless he can relate it to something outside himself; unless, that is, he can belong to something in cosmos. He is indeed a homeless wanderer; by identifying himself with steel, he can draw strength from the feeling that it is he who keeps the ship moving. This illusion, however, does not take long to be shattered. He is rejected by Mildred Douglas and then by the rich of Fifth Avenue. He joins the anarchist organization only to realize that his place is not there either. He is hauled off to prison. When, however, he comes out, he is broken and disconsolate. The protagonist of Hemingway struggles to the last moment. Even when Jordan sustains a bullet injury, neither his beloved nor the Guerrillas are ready to leave him in the lurch. Pain that the bullet injury gives him is unbearable. Still, he does not yield. The only desire of his heart is to dispatch some of his enemies to death before he dies. This establishes the truth that the protagonist of Hemingway can smile in the face of death and does not hesitate to act in order to assert his self. Active self is the only solution to all the turmoil of human life. This ideology is again and again reiterated in Hemingway's novels.

5

Being and Becoming

Man, today, is at the crossroads of utter confusion, in fact, at a loss to decide as to what course of action should be taken in the face of harsher realities of life. The erosion of ethical and social values and the occurrence of the devastating world wars shocked man into the loss of his self: "I was /I no more exist."[142] Human beings lost faith in executing worthy actions to realize their 'self'. Naturally, life has been reduced to what T.S.Eliot calls "...a hundred visions and revisions, before taking of a toast and tea."[143] It is this loss of vitality in life to realize the 'self' that has bred existential anxiety. The French existentialist philosopher Kierkegaard, Satre, Camus and others, too, try to explore existential agony of 'self'. Kierkegaard arrives at a religious consolation and relishes his true 'self' in the belief that "God is transcendental; almighty ... it can be felt within."[144] But, the exploration of Satre and Camus ends in despair. They will fail to evolve any faith, which may organize human life and satisfy 'self'. The result is the complete loss of one's self and the tragic experience of nothingness:

> I am self -consumer of my woes -
>
> They rise and vanish in oblivious host,
>
> Like shadows in love's frenzied, stifled throes;

> And yet I am and alive -like vapour toast
> Into the nothingness of scorn and noise
> Into the living sea of waking dreams,
> Where there is neither sense of life or joys,
> But the vast ship wreck of my life esteems:[145]

Camus, too, in his novel The Outsider depicts the terrible confusion and meaninglessness that have overtaken human life. The protagonist fails to comprehend his own 'self'. Moreover, he becomes an outsider -an outsider to God, to Nature, and to gigantic social apparatus, that supplies his natural wants. But the worst form of experience is his "alienation from his own self."[146] K in Kafka's The Trial is no less an alienated protagonist. This is as truer of Gregor Samsa in The Metamorphosis. He awakens one morning to find himself transformed into an insect. He becomes estranged not only from his family members, but also, from his own 'self'. What is common in all these existential characters is the loss of their 'self'. Strindberg, who Eugene O'Neill calls "the precursor of all modernity in our present theatre"[147] is so much shocked at the loss of 'self' that he considers the state of belligerency between the partners of life -man and woman -a perfectly normal feature of human life. In his play The Father, the dramatist presents a picture of a husband who, heading towards a catastrophe, says to his inexorable spouse:

> If it's true we have descended from ape, it must have been from two different species. There's no likeness between us.[148]

The way he talks shows that he is a creature neither of a world with a settled values of life nor knowing his real 'self'. Luigi Pirandello has no better comfort to offer. In fact, he bases his logic of man's loss of self on philosophical grounds. He feels that if a Man is mystery to others, so is he to himself. Since the world expects him to become frozen in a fixed from, he solidifies his daily life around some stereotype supplied to him, closing his eyes to the incessant change and flux of time that is challenging as much his inner world as the outer one. It is this experience which makes Ted Hughes say:

> The sun is behind me
>
> Nothing has changed since I began
>
> My eye has permitted no change
>
> I am going to keep things like this.[149]

Therefore, it is this terrible experience of the loss of self, and the incapacity to struggle for realizing the existence of the same that have generated existential anxiety in the modern world.

Ernest Hemingway explores the existential anxiety of the age, and nihilistic fervour spreading over the world. In the words of Spiller, he

> "denied the denial. Ruthless probing to the depths of human predicament had discovered an unsuspected rock bottom. The will to live was there, and beyond it, as Faulkner was later to assert so defiantly in his Nobel Prize address, the will to prevail. On this basis the art could be built."[150]

Hemingway's first step towards his aim of encountering existential problems is to accept reality as it is. In other words, he does not want illusions or dreams to be a refuge for escaping from the hard realities of life. Eugene O'Neill in The Ice Man Cometh shows that men from different walks of life are so horrified by the existential cruelty that they take asylum in pipe-dreams. Tennessee Williams in his play The Glass Menagerie and A Street Named Desire shows how illusions are being nursed to escape from existential agony. But, Hemingway asks people to follow the religion of reality and hard facts.

"So live in it and never know it", writes Hemingway in his story A Clean Well Lighted Place, "was all a nothing and a man was nothing too."[151] Here, the artist is exhorting the people to gain awareness of reality which may ultimately lead him to the realization of 'self'. This fact has found an artistic presentation in his novel The Sun Also Rises. Here, he depicts the life-style of human beings who have lost the sense of real purpose of life on earth. Their life has become mechanical. T.S.Eliot aptly describes the emptiness of human values in his poem 'The Love Song of J. Alfred Prufrock':

> In the room the women come and go
>
> Talking of Michelangelo.[152]

The women described in the poem have nothing to do except moving hither and thither leisurely and talking of the great Italian painter Michelangelo. Brett is a lady whose main occupation is to enjoy sexual pleasures with rich and smart young men. At times, she is seen enjoying the company of Cohn, Count Mippipopolous and at times, she is seen making love with Romero, Mike and Jake. Cohn is an indecisive and flippant fellow. He divorces his first wife, and gets engaged with another lady. But, as he comes across Brett, he madly hankers after hurt. Mike, who is engaged to Brett, is a sentimental fool. He drinks over his head to ward-off the shocks that he receives due to the licentious behavior of his would-be-wife. Jake is an impotent man. But, his interest lies in roaming from one club to another with one woman another, and studying the character of Brett. Thus, Hemingway very vividly shows the life of rootless characters indifferent to their real 'self', and living a life on the plane of superficiality. The whole episode reminds us of Eliot's "The Waste Land" where Eliot says:

> Unreal city,
>
> Under the brown fog of a winter dawn,
>
> A crowd flowed over London Bridge, so many,
>
> I had not thought death had undone so many.[153]

Here, 'death' means the failure to recognize the real meaning of life, and loss of 'self' of human beings.

Hemingway tries to show how the vitality of life is now a spent-force. All the characters go to Spain where Fiesta is being celebrated. Fiesta means bull fighting. The bloody and hair-raising duel between a matador and bull actuates a man to the awareness of the immense potentialities of life. But, here, all the characters, except Jake, remain enveloped in their daydream activities. Cohn is always engaged in perusing Brett. Mike is all the time drunk. Brett herself is engaged in spreading a net to entrap Romero, a young bullfighter, in her love. The irony of the novelist is pretty clear. The existential agony of the modern world is so poignant that the people like to live a cold and passive life, and reveal in it, for

> Winter kept us warm, covering
> Earth in forgetful snow.[154]

But, Jake finally comes to realize his own idiocy in living in fool's paradise. When he returns to San Sabastian from Spain to relax and ruminate over his actions in public and private life, he gets equipped with a sense of self-realization. He does not bully himself about his admiration for Brett or her inconstancy. Naturally, when he receives a telegram from Brett to rescue her from pecuniary crisis, he cannot help mocking at her ignorance. He sends her a telegram, and feels "That seems to handle it."[155] The indifferent tone of expression highlights his gradual enlightenment. This becomes more specific, when Brett is shown going in a taxi with Jake. She tells Jake "O Jake, we could have had such a good time together."[156] Now, life has become 'could have had'. This small but very striking expression reminds us of D.G.Rossetti who says:

> Look in my face: my name is Might have been;
> I am also called No-more, Too-late, Farewell;
> Upon thine ear I hold the dead-sea shell
> Cast up thy life a foam-fretted feet between;[157]

Therefore, life in modern times has become 'could have had' or 'might have been'. Spiller suggests:

> The normal world was already a world of might have been. Now it was only a good time -a phrase capable of interpretation on any level from the highest to the lowest -it was intensity alone that they were seeking and that they found feelingly in frantic love-making, in death, in bullring, on Martin after Martin.[158]

But, Hemingway makes Jake perceive the hollowness of Brett's assertion. Therefore, he remarks: "Yes ... . Isn't it pretty to think so?"[159] It is here that Jake is seen mocking at the illusory and make belief worlds of young men who are trying tooth and nail to escape from the dragon-net of reality. Hemingway argues against this sort of life. This becomes crystal clear in his second novel A Farewell to Arms.

In A Farewell to Arms Hemingway has once again denounced illusions as Utopian ideals meant to escape from the existential anxiety of self. The protagonist of the novel, Henry who is in the army, nurses a false opinion about life in war and in love. He says:

> Well I knew I would not be killed. Not in this war. It did not have anything to do with me. It seemed no more dangerous to me myself than war in the movies.[160]

He is completely given to sensual pleasures and intoxicating liquors. The emptiness inside the self of Henry runs parallel with outside self. Love from Catherine to Henry is but a sub game. Henry entertains a soldier's motto of loving them and leaving them:

> I knew I did not love Catherine Barkley, nor had any idea of loving her. This was a game like a bridge in which you said things instead of playing cards. Like Bridge you had to pretend you were

> playing for money or playing for some stakes. Nobody had been shown what the stakes were. It was a right with me.[161]

The emotional out-burst of Catherine who has suffered a setback at the death of her previous lover is merely a sign of eccentricity for Henry. Hemingway, from the existential point of view, is very pertinent in ironizing this behavior of the protagonist who, like many teenage Americans of the lost generation, is living in a make-belief world of romance and adventure. Hemingway's attitude comes near to that of Eugene O'Neill who in The Icemen Cometh shows people belonging to different walks of life taking refuge in 'pipe-dreams' to dilute their existential anxiety. Though Henry is unconsciously living in a make-belief world of romance, yet Hemingway makes no concession in administering shocks to make him realize the existential realities of life -that all the human relationships are bound to shatter and dream world collapse.

The realization of the horrors of war descends upon Henry when he gets injured by a mortar shell. When he is hit, he finds that he is really in the war after all.

> I tried to breathe but my breath would not come and I felt myself rush bodily out of myself and out and out .... .[162]

The hair-raising deaths of his colleagues and pitiable condition of the injured soldiers awaken him to reality. Henry, like Major Serjius in Arms and the Man, comes to realize the difference between chivalric vision of war and actual war. At once, he is overtaken by existential anxiety. But, he takes refuge in the love of Catherine to escape from the shocks of the grim realities of life. In fact, he is merely creating another illusion of living a blessed life with Catherine. When he is admitted into the hospital of Milan, his association with Catherine takes a new turn. "When I saw her I was in love with her."[163] Their love grows so strong and close that their commitment to each other does not need any social sanction:

> There is no way to be married except by church or state.
>
> We are married privately. You see, darling, it would mean everything to me if I had any religion. But I haven't any religion.
>
> 'You game me the Saint Anthony.'
>
> 'That was for luck. Someone gave it to me.'
>
> 'Then nothing worries you?'
>
> "Only being sent away from you. You're my religion.'
>
> 'You're all I've got.'[164]

Again, Henry starts nursing a desire to escape with Catherine to a place where no human interference is possible and where they can enjoy a life of perpetual bliss. He runs away from the Italian front of war and escapes with Catherine to Switzerland. The police or the secret agents of Italy fail to arrest Henry. But the question remains -can life be enjoyed in perpetual bliss as Tennyson says 'the whole I dream a dream of good' or spent happily in love with a lady as Arnold says 'Ah love! Let us be true to one another?' Hemingway knows that these are only temporal measure to dilute the existential anxiety coercing the self of man. Naturally, at the end, Catherine dies during childbirth and Henry is left alone. It is in this way that Hemingway directs his protagonists to realize the real essence of the existence of life on earth:

> With her death Frederic Henry, the new Hemingway Everyman, is left in strange land, alone and without direction. Wounded and haunted by his own inadequacy, he had known love and death; bound to the level plane, he had finally discovered

> and had sought the mountains. Even though he might never learn to climb, he could not now die by his own hand.[165]

Hemingway's hero accepts the realities as they are and confidently goes out to face life with all its pain and suffering:

> But after I had got them out and shut the door and turned off the light it wasn't any good. It was like saying goodbye to a statue. After a while I went out and left the hospital and walked back to the hotel in the rain.[166]

This is how existential anxiety should be faced and the self asserted.

In his another novel For Whom the Bell Tolls, Hemingway's vision of existential problem is present in an epic magnitude. The protagonist, Jordan is in possession of the knowledge about temporal human relationships and inevitable extinction of life. He has to blow a bridge with the help of a band of Guerrillas. He knows that his own life and those of Guerrillas would be jeopardized in the accomplishment of the mission. Moreover, he develops a very close relationship with Maria who has remained 'selfless' even by continued tyranny of the fascists. The other members of the Guerrilla's party -Anselmo, El Sordo, Pilar and others -develop a profound relationship with Jordan. Hemingway has very artistically brought into focus one of the most universal existential problems -whether the true existence of self lies in the pursuit of one's own welfare and ambition or in the sacrifice of one's personal ambition and happiness for something universal. The novelists like Jean Stafford and Fitzgerald show their protagonists leading a life with no other ambition but personal gain. Fitzgerald, in his novel The Last Tycoon, shows the kind of the spiritual predicament a man meets by leading a life based on purely personal plane. The protagonist Monroe puts up a tough fight against the anonymous controllers of the movie industry and the growing strength of the employees. His life is spent on no grand purpose. Naturally, his shocks in life and tragic death have no significance in the spectrum of human destiny. Jordan, too, like Monroe wants to live a life of ordinary human beings with Maria as his wife:

> Alright they would have two rooms and she could do what she liked while he went up there and he'd come back from Graylord's to her, she had waited up in the hills all that time she could wait a little while at the hotel Florida.[167]

Jordan seems to be allured by the rosy prospect of his life with Maria as we have seen Henry, in A Farewell to Arms, thinking about his life with Catherine.

But, Hemingway does not allow Jordan to meet the fate of Henry. Though he knows that war has many limitations, yet the cause for which he fights is dear to him. The impossibility and the risk of the mission gradually pale into insignificance. He indulges in a self-debate:

> Yes, he should carry them out because it is only in the performing of them that they can prove to be impossible. How do you know they are impossible until you have tried them? If everyone said orders were impossible to carry out when they were received where would you be? Where would we all be if you just said, Impossible when orders came.[168]

This self-debate opens a new vision of life before Jordan and he gets ready to sacrifice all for the cause he is fighting for liberation of human beings from the Fascists who stand for human servitude and slavery. 'No, there was nothing to be gained by leaving them alone.'[169] Hemingway is emphasizing that the true existence of 'self' lies in fighting for some universal cause. Albert Camus in his novel The Plague shows Dr. Rieux fighting with the plague which has engulfed an 'Algerian coastal city of Oran'[170]. Two other prominent characters Tarrou and Rambert also toil to save people from becoming the victims of plague. Rambert ardently desires to escape from the city to meet his mistress and live in his own country. But, Tarrou is ready to sacrifice all his happiness for helping people in this crisis. He is confident to win over the plague -a universal cause. Gradually, Rambert, too, comes to realize that true happiness lies in sacrificing one's own happiness for something universal:

> ' "Yes", said Rambert, "but there may be something to be ashamed of in being happy by oneself." '
>
> 'Tarrou ... pointed out that if Rambert wished to share the unhappiness of man he would never have time again for happiness. He would have to choose.'
>
> ' "It's not that", said Rambert "I always thought that I was a stranger in this town and that I had nothing to do with you. But now that I have seen what I have seen I know that I belong to this place whether I like it or not. This business concerns us all." '[171]

Tarrou dies of plague and the doctor starts speculating whether the former has won the game or not. However, a very realistic sensibility comes to him:

> All that man could win in the game of plague and life was knowledge and memory. Perhaps it was that that Tarrou called "winning".[172]

It is in this sort of fight or undaunted struggle that the existence of the real 'self' of man can be realized. Hemingway shows Jordan giving up his own life and his own happiness for the cause he is fighting.

> It is all figured out guapa, he said softly against Maria's shoulder ... . We'll be killed but we'll blow the bridge.[173]

This is what happens. In the course of blowing the

bridge and making an escape from the site, he is fatally injured. He feels that if he would go along with them, the security of all the members might get endangered. Though Agustin, Pablo, Primitivo and others are ready to carry him, yet he voluntarily resolves to be left alone. He persuades Maria to go away. When he is alone with a loaded machinegun, the ever increasing pain kindles a desire in him to commit suicide. But, Hemingway's hero quickly puts off the idea. He has the consolation of accomplishing his action for the cause. Unlike the protagonists of Doss Passos, Henry Miller and Fitzgerald, Jordan meets the end of his life very confidently, for he has realized the true existence of his 'self'. He is not assailed by the meaninglessness of his life or futility of his action as we find in the case of modern existential characters:

> He looked down the hill slope again and he thought, I hate to leave it, that is all. I hate to leave it very much and I hope I have done some good in it. I have tried to with what talent I had ... . I have fought for what I believed in ....[174]

He dies after shoting down the officer persuing the Guerrillas. But his death does not issue out any nihilistic effect:

> He loves Maria, he blows up his bridge, he meets a meaningless death in flight; but he has heard the bell toll he can die thinking, 'One thing well done can make ....'[175]

Thus, Hemingway shows that existential agony of 'self' is averted by pursuing aa universal cause. This is what we see in Samuel Beckett's Waiting for Godot. For the time Vladimir and Estragon are concerned with their miserable plight, their 'self' seems to have no meaning. But, as soon as they identify themselves with the whole humanity, their 'self' gains a meaningful existence. Therefore, we see a latent force in the assertion of Vladimir:

> Let us do something, while we have the chance! It is not every day that we are needed. Not indeed that we personally are needed. Others would meet the case equally well, if not better .... But at this place, at this moment of time, all mankind is us .... .[176]

In the same manner, Hemingway sees the existence of 'self' in the light of a broad humanitarian concern rather than personal loyalty. The protagonist of For Whom the Bell Tolls is suffused with a sense of involvement in the lives and sufferings of others. He is willing to lay down his life for the eventual happiness of the Spanish people. John Donne has written:

> ... any man's death diminishes me, because I am involved in Mankinds; and therefore never send to know for whom the bell tolls; It tolls for thee.[177]

This sermon of Donne amply illustrates that humanitarian perspective of life can assuge existential anxiety of 'self' because 'Bell tolls for thee'.

The existential question has been explored in the most intensive manner in the last novel of Ernest Hemingway entitled The Old Man And The Sea. This 'self' of an individual can exist only by making a Jordan-like commitment and translating it into reality. This has been presented in a concrete fashion in The Old Man And The Sea. The old man, Santiago, has not been able to catch even a single fish for the last eighty-four days. Other fishermen jeer at his failure. This old man is a symbol of modern individual who is deemed to be bankrupt of all valour and stamina. Cast out by a success-driven society, he temporarily loses his self-poise; for a destabilization of the individual's achieved status inevitably depletes his self-belief. So, revealing his self-alienation, the old man cries out, "I have no luck anymore".[178] But, his resilient mettle soon asserts itself and he proclaims, "I may not be as strong as I think ... . But I many tricks and I have resolution".[179] Since a fisherman can redeem his honour only by making the fishing voyage successful, the next day he rose out far into the sea, with hope and determination in order to reestablish himself. Eliot has very artistically presented the picture of a 'selfless' modern man sitting hopelessly:

> Here I am, an old man in a dry month,
>
> Being read to by a boy; waiting for rain.[180]

Beckett, too, presents Vladimir and Estragon in Waiting for Godot as unconscious about the very existence of their self. The vacuum that they experience in their life comes to the fore, when Estragon says: "Nothing happens, nobody comes, nobody goes, it's awful!"[181] But Hemingway has adopted a different attitude towards the problem of the existence of 'self'. The old man is not hopeless and paralyzed. He is true to his commitment. He goes out into the sea with confidence to catch fishes everyday with the idea:

> But, he thought, I keep them with precision. Only I have no luck anymore. But who knows? May be today. Everyday is a new day. It is better to be lucky. But I would rather be exact. Then when luck comes you are ready.[182]

The rising sun is painful to the eyes of the old man. But, "All my life the early sun has hurt my eyes, he thought yet they are still good."[183] He encounters all the obstacles of life with perfect ease and composure. All the time, the old man is pensively on the lookout for a big fish:

> Now is no time to think of baseball, he thought. Now is the time to think of only one thing. That which I was born for. There might be a big one around that school, he thought.[184]

Once on the sea, Santiago meticulously performs the fisherman's skills. Though he hopes for a better 'luck' this time round, he "would rather be exact".[185] He even dares to pit himself against the mighty sea by 'crowd'-ing the 'current a little' in order to 'fish' correctly. Here, Santiago's professionalism and daring highlight his incontrovertible difference from the shallow water fishermen who "let them (the fishing lines) drift with the current",[186] and tamely submit to the vagaries of the sea. For him, the life of land means doing nothing –an unbearable passivity; but the sea rouses the male in him. His perseverance eventually bears fruit, and 'luck' comes his way when his bait is taken by something 'unbelievably heavy' –'a marlin'. He hooks the huge fish, and an epic struggle ensues between the predator and the prey.

The old man catches a big fish, but he has to face tremendous problems in the process of killing it. After the continuous struggle with the fish for two nights, he succeeds in killing her. The struggle that the old man indulges in makes his palms bleed, body exhausted and his force, toned down. In spite of all this, the old man strives to keep his mind composed. Shunning stray thoughts like 'baseball' and 'radio', he concentrates hard on the job at hand. He knows that he will have to kill the fish, regardless of his great 'love' and 'respect' for it.

> 'Keep my head clear', he said against the wood of the bow. 'I am a tired old man. But I have killed this fish which is my brother and now I must do the slave work.'[187]

The old man's 'will' and 'intelligence' finally make him win the day. He wins a problematic individual 'victory' albeit on the psychological plane. He returns to the shore, physically routed but succeeds in justifying his 'self-image' because he has 'killed this fish,"[188] and 'killed him well'"[189]. He is delighted to think that even the great Di Maggio would be proud of him after this episode. The sense of triumph dominates over the physical debacle and is contrasted with his psychological elevation. It provides him the energy to work and act with grace under pressure. Right from the beginning it may be witnessed with clarity that he imposes his will over the circumstances which are of course beyond control. Stanley Cooperman records this unflinching zeal:

> Santiago is indeed timeless; an aged monument to that power of will which finally emerges as the only means to defeat age itself, he remains a monument that stands for and by nothing but its own existence.[190]

As an aggressive individual, who he remains throughout in the novel does not only posses courage to fight with the impossible in order to make that possible but also lives by a vision. It suggests that he does not fear even to risk his own life, for it is' a means of attaining meaning of life. 'Death' or 'life' is insignificant before the dignity of man. Therefore, he presses the panic button :when the same is due to create an impact of existence. If we look into the character of Santiago from this perspective, it is evident that he suffers like a man showing the impregnality of spirit which is always a paramount motif of his personality. For an individual to be the victim in natural struggle is no disgrace if he fights well according to his abilities. To lose in the long run is inevitable. But the noble creatures in the story transcend defeat by displaying intense life at the moment of death. The basic action and timelessness of a parable simply convey a meaningful image of moral heroism. He is a simple but strange old man who is capable of an extraordinary dignity and heroism by means of which he wins a moral triumph in the midst of what is otherwise a heart-breaking defeat. Bickford Sylvester while investigating Santiago's 'strange'-ness surmises:

> Santiago is strange because he is in every material sense "the real old man" Hemingway later called him. He is real like us, yet he behaves and thinks -with remarkable regularity -as we are able to behave and think only in our very best moments.

> And that is exalting to us, because he is human; he is possible.[191]

The old man's luckless voyage symbolizes the struggle between man and nature with the ancient bonds between hunters and hunted. Respecting his prey, the hunter must nevertheless assert at any price the power of man. He attains supreme position in the hearts of many by killing the fish and killing it well. In fact, these are small wonders especially when we consider his humiliating defeat before the giant marlin. But in the process when he proclaims "man cannot be destroyed" attains the highest honour for showing exemplary courage to remain upbeat till the last breath. Santiago's fierce individualism is finally reconciled to the passivity of the shallow water fishermen. Sylvester asserts:

> There is indeed in The Old Man And The Sea a greater tolerance shown toward the total community than ever before in Hemingway's work... . But rather than interdependence, there is implied the dependence upon a principle basic to universal order, is independent of all men.[192]

There is a gradual shift in his personality trying to adjust itself or rather appropriate the same in order to establish the existence of the self. Peter Berger calls it a 'shift from traditional to modern identity.[193] This is where the old man seen to slope off the 'world of honour' in which the 'individual discovers his true identity by liberating his persona from his socially imposed roles.[194] Undoubtedly it makes him an entity in the society whose actions are louder than voice. Much in keeping Alain Touraine's theory of 'actionalism', Santiago becomes a social actor.[195] Though disappointed for becoming a simple 'component' of the social system, he tries to be an 'agent' of that system.[196] Such an act of man takes him to the pedestal of glory. Probably that is the reason why Arvin R. Wells calls the old man 'the apotheosis of the code hero.[197] Therefore when Wells says, 'His experience is not only a confirmation of personal dignity and courage but what is perhaps best called a ritual of transfiguration', [198] aptly justifies the same in case of Santiago, for he personifies the personality.

In fact, when we put Santiago along with all other significant characters, he stands apart because in him perhaps we find Hemingway's enduring concern with the co-existence and intersection between the 'human world' and the 'natural world'. It becomes reciprocal especially in a situation like this because their co-existence is proximate and thus allowing to have intimate and complex interactions. The novel clearly showcases two kinds of feelings—one the natural world of the sea bewilders us with its unpredictable responses of 'give'-ing and 'withhold'-ing, and the other, the human world, which seems strangely divided into the passive community of shallow water fishermen and the potent redeemer Santiago. Therefore, when Santiago is compared to his viscounts, his 'strange'-ness is certainly licensed. He is gifted with an all-embracing view of the human condition impervious by the limits of percept and example. It is in the fitness of things both the novelist and the protagonist too perceives that man is caught in an alienated state thus but both are equally ready to make due allowances for the human will to success and dignity. Incidentally, it is through the protagonist that Hemingway seems to 'connect' with what his contemporary William Faulkner said in his Nobel Prize acceptance speech, 'man will not merely endure: he will prevail'.

Hemingway shows that true commitment and hopeful attitude are necessary for realization of true 'self'. In Waiting for Godot, too, Vladimir and Estragon have hope that the arrival of Godot would end all their miseries in life. They indulge in meaningless activities to pass-off time. By opening shoes, putting off hats, jumping and abusing each other, they try to ward off the feeling of boredom that is obsessing their 'self'. But, while Vladimir and Estragon are different and depressed, the old man is always confident and hopeful.

Hemingway has already shown in For Whom the Bell Tolls that the existence of 'self' of an individual lies in merely striving for accomplishing a commitment, for a commitment is an ideal which is never achieved. As the old man is returning with the fish, the sharks pounce upon it's flesh. Once again, the old man renews his efforts to fight with the sharks. Though the night dims his eyesight, yet he continues to save his fish: 'Fight them', he said. 'I'll fight them until I die.'[199] But by the mid night, he comes to understand that the fight is useless, for the fish has been eaten by the sharks. It is a heart-breaking blow to the old man. The commitment made by the old man gets fractured, yet he is defiant in his attitude: "He spat into the ocean" and said, "Eat that, Galanos. And make a dream you've killed a man."[200] He consoles himself 'Nothing', he said aloud. "I went out too far."[201] This is the way the 'self' of an individual exists. It does not matter whether one succeeds in the game of life or not, what matters is whether or not the game has been played confidently and honestly. In Waiting for Godot, too, Vladimir and Estragon get convinced that Godot will never come. Still, they wait. It is in this act of waiting and hoping that the existence of 'self' is realized. Vladimir says with pride:

> We have kept our appointment, and that's an end to that. We are not saints, but we have kept our appointment. how many people can boast as much?[202]

Both Hemingway and Beckett tackle the existential problem in the same way. They suggest that commitment should be made and it should be followed with confidence, though the result may be depressing and disappointing.

Thus, one sees that Hemingway has tried to cope with the problem of existential anxiety of the modern world in a very systematized manner. At first, in The Sun Also Rises and A Farewell to Arms, he emphasizes the indispensability of accepting the stark and painful realities of the world confidently. In the next novel For Whom the Bell Tolls, he propounds that one can realize the existence of 'self' by making a commitment beyond one's self. But, in the fourth novel The Old Man And The Sea -his vision of the existence of 'self' is widened and is firmly rooted in the realities of daily life. Every individual should pursue the commitment, personal or impersonal, that he has made and it is in this pursuit that the existence of 'self' can be realized and action can be taken. This is the perennial philosophy of life.

6

Conclusion: Dynamics of Eclectic Perfection

> I decline to accept the end of men ... I believe that man will not merely endure: he will prevail. He is immortal not because he alone among creatures has an inexhaustible voice but because he has a soul, a spirit capable of compassion and sacrifice and endurance.
>
> –William Faulkner

Hemingway's novels have been an odyssey of 'self' and their tenor a positive, dynamic, active stance of life. In this age of excessive intellectual exploration and brutal warfare, sustaining human values have fallen apart. Different artists have responded in different fashions to these incidents. Eliot and Yeats utilize myths to forge a pattern out of an apparently disorganized life where selfhood of man was lost. Eliot has written:

> "In face of any naturally horrifying phenomenon like war we must measure the suffering, direct or indirect, against the spiritual good which may come of suffering. We may find that the proportion of futile suffering, and of that kind of suffering which

> makes men worse rather than better, which abates their human dignity and deadens their sense of responsibility, is far too high; and that the total effect is at best one of futility."[203]

W.B.Yeats, in his poem 'The Second Coming' uses the image of falcon. The falcon is out of the control of the falconer suggesting that humanity itself was at the point of crumbling. The centre could not hold as a result of which things fell apart. Everything was in a state of chaos and confusion. The falcon cannot hear the falconer;

> "Turning and turning in the widening gyre,
>
> The falcon cannot hear the falconer,
>
> Things fall apart; the center cannot hold;
>
> Mere anarchy is loosed upon the world."[204]

Artists like Newman and Conrad Aiken stick to religious sentiments for diffusing the crisis of self and encounter futility:

> It is to self you come,—
>
> And that is God. It is the seed of seeds.[205]

Huxley and Baudelaire make an in depth exploration of the decaying and nauseating conditions of life on earth. But, these artists seem to have a limited appeal to the people at large. This is because Eliot and Yeats become highly intellectual. Huxley creates a façade of satire and fantasy. Baudelaire becomes morbid and repulsive. Newman and Aiken are orthodoxical. Therefore, their appeal is limited to the selective classes of the society. The majority of the people felt victim to the de-humanizing tendencies of the modern world. Earth with all its aggrandizement and progress seems to be a place of glorious uncertainties. The conditions are vividly explained by Arnold in Dover Beach:

> Lie before, us like a land of dreams

> So various, so beautiful and so new
> Hath really neither joy nor love nor light
> Nor certitude, nor peace, nor help for pain.
> And we are here as on a darkling plain
> Swept with confused alarms of struggle and flight
> Where ignorant armies clash by night.[206]

It is at this juncture that Hemingway makes an appearance on the world arena, and ventilates a fresh breeze of enthusiasm and zeal in the hearts of depressed humanity to assert their 'self'.

Hemingway has not explored life with any intellectual realities of life. What he has in common with the general humanity is the acute experience of "complete loss of faith in practically any of the traditional values, an awareness of violence and death."[207] Naturally, he sets out in a journey to assert 'self' under the changed circumstances:

> His apparent loss of faith is counterbalanced by a more honest statement on the workings of basic appetites of Man, of the craving for food and drink, and sexual satisfaction.[208]

His exploration of 'self' by actuating the dormant potentialities of man endears him to the majority of the readers of the post-war period.

'Sex' lost all its creative power by the continued experiments to live a free, natural and nomadic life, and by the excess of intellectual growth. Hemingway has chosen an intermediate path. He makes 'sex' a basic ingredient of the life of human beings; it actuates man towards a positive direction. But, 'sex' according to Hemingway, is of such immense value that it entails honesty and constancy between the partners. For Henry, Morgan and Jordan, 'sex' proves to be a major exhorting force which makes them face the crude realities of life with confidence and honour. Therefore, Hemingway makes a bare appetite of human (sex) an inexhaustible source of creative energy and power.

In modern circumstances, all human relationships and mutual love which guided an individual towards the development of his 'self' have been shattered to pieces. An individual has become a lone, insignificant entity in the crowd. Hemingway has explored the tragic condition of a lone man in a very realistic fashion. Though, he emphasizes the necessity of solidarity in To Have And Have Not and For Whom the Bell Tolls, yet during the fag end of his literary career he changes his viewpoint. In the last scene of For Whom the Bell Tolls, he very pertinently observes: "The people cannot go together. Each one must do it alone."[209] In The Old Man And The Sea, Hemingway pinpoints the necessity to prepare one's self to fight with the odds of life without asking a helping hand. The old man says to himself: "You better be fearless and confident yourself, old man."[210] The real 'self' of man lies in combating with the antagonistic forces of the world alone, and confidently.

The fear of death has been generated by the brutal massacre and annihilation of human life in the scientific warfare. This fear has been so enormous and acute that modern man has become a 'selfless' being. No religious value or myth can eradicate this fear-complex settled in the consciousness of human beings. But, Hemingway prescribes a very simple and rewarding diagnosis. He advocates for aggressive life -a life lived in constant company of hair-raising and risky situations of life. It is in this way only that the real intensity of life, and 'self' of man can be realized:

> His awareness of death and role of violence in human existence of coupled with a profound feeling for the intensity of life.[211]

It is this awareness of death and violence in life which makes a man enjoy the intensity of self. The sense of nothingness crippled and forced human beings to live a passive and inactive life. In a drama of Beckett, Play, we see characters lying encased in urns, for there is no scope of living an active life in the world. Some artists like Eugene O'Neill and Tennessee Williams invent pipe-dreams to escape from the painful experience of hollowness and morbidity of actual life. But, Hemingway preaches a religion of hard facts and cruel realities of life. He exhorts people to accept and face reality that mitigates the sense of nothingness. Further, he demands that every human being should make a commitment, and strive to achieve it. Though Hemingway is very specific on the point that commitment is never fully achieved. Yet he suggests that human dignity and test of self lies in striving for it honestly and perpetually. Jordan's commitment is to blow the bridge. He accomplishes his mission. It hardly matters whether he remains alive after the execution of his mission or not.

> Now finally and at last, there was no problem. However all of it had been and however, all of it would ever be now, for him, no longer was there any problem.[212]

The old man, Santiago, too dreams of lion even after losing his fish that he caught after daring struggle. Santiago has done his task. Therefore, it does not matter whether he gets positive result or not. But, the fact remains, Santiago has realized his 'self' and enjoyed the intensity of life.

Therefore, Hemingway has been acknowledged as an outstanding artist who made a successful attempt to adduce such principles of life as may make human beings assert their 'self'. His novels are exploration of this real and aggressive self of man. Therefore, Hemingway has been called:

> ... the bronze god of the whole contemporary literary experience in America.[213]

Therefore, it becomes clear that it is he who, starting from a basically disillusioned attitude bordering on nihilism, proceeded to evolve new values which enlightened the 'self' of man.

Running through Ernest Hemingway's work, from In Our Time to The Old Man And The Sea, are two dominant motifs –the matador and the crucified. The matador represents a great force held in check, releasing itself proudly in a controlled yet violent administering of death. The crucified stands for the taking of pain, even unto death, with all of one's courage and endurance. So, not until The Old Man And The Sea, Hemingway achieved a perfect blending of his two themes, the continual tension and interplay between those forces represented Hemingway canon against which the individual works of fiction may be profitably studied.

In Our Time sets forth the pain and brutality of our world, recorded apparently without comment in a terse, telegraphic style. Yet underneath the tight-lipped writing a current of protest and repressed brooding threads its secretive way. This is violence caught in the stifled shock of its initial impact. The stories and interchapters have the effect of painful memories of which he must rid himself to exercise their evil spell, to drive them from the night into the day.

Recoiling from these memories of a sick world, the discharged soldier Nick Adams sought retreat in the Big Two -Hearted River. In this story, Hemingway omits rather ominously all mention of the war and of the people and places of Nick's past, so that a strange aloneness and suspension of time are created. Nick's only function was to fish, to immerse himself so completely in the physical sensations and details of his fishing that there was no need to think. This became, therefore, a strange idyll. Nick called it 'the good place', but it was the good place because of its associations with a certain part of his past –fishing and hunting, the river and the woods –which had not been exercised from his life as he was trying to do with all the rest. It was as though he wanted to rub out his immediate past and begin clean again here in the woods. But even the woods had been burned over –now there were just charred stumps and black grass hoppers. Yet here amid the shelter and quiet of the trees and the river, with the sun warm on his back and his line trailing in the water, was a moment of separation, of forgetfulness, of peace.

If Nick Adams was trying to withdraw from his world in "Big Two-Hearted River", it was in "Soldier's Home" that the Hemingway protagonist was officially separated. The soldier Krebs found himself hopelessly alienated from the conventional, middle-class American town to which he returned. Living with a kind of flat despair from day-to-day, holding in abeyance the inevitable decision, he dwelt in uneasy isolation in the midst of his family. Pushed to action finally by family pressure, he decided to sever the last clinging thread of his filial bond. It was a curiously cold, passionless rebellion, as though he had long since worn our his emotions and given up his hope.

In cutting the human bonds that tie, one to his world there is the danger of cutting into the very will to live. The threat of this infection hovers over the three stories "Mr. and Mrs. Elliot", "Cat in the Rain", and "Out of Season", each concerned with an American couple characterized by sexual sterility and impotence. Marked by a strangely bloodless discard, without intensity or love, their lives follow a drifting purposeless course. But like green wooded mountains rising abruptly out of barren plains, the descriptions of matadors emerge in sharp relief.

From the unvoiced fears of disintegration of Nick Adams, from the weary despair apathy of Krebs, and from the scorn, which may mask a secret dread, of the passionless and sterile union of impotent lovers, Hemingway has turned to the violence of the matador.

The theme is developed more fully in The Sun Also Rises. If In Our Time recorded, for Hemingway, the waves of man's violence effacing the recognizable outline of the shore of one's home, The Sun Also Rises depicts the human wreckage that had been left behind. In The Sun Also Rises, four or five men go on an expedition to Spain to see a bull-fight, along with an English lady, who is a desperate nymphomaniac. This lady named Brett falls in love with one named Jake who unfortunately, has been physically incapacitated in the war. The lady is obliged, in order to satisfy her imperious needs, to take for lover now one, now another of his companions. The last one is so much in love with her that he asks her to marry him. But she turns out to be a woman of honour. She realizes that her lover is much younger than she and hence she determines not to ruin his life. It is a fine occasion for sentimental heroics. But Hemingway refuses life to its simplest elements. And there are physical movements; heat, cold, thirst, sleepiness, pain and the like. On the subjective side, he admits the fun of fishing, watching a bull-fight and such simple states as "feeling fine". The novel pictures the American expatriates in Europe. The time was one of the irresponsibility, drunkenness, and promiscuity. As Mike pursued his drunken way, trailing his mounting debts like a banner, Brett preceded her escort, trailing her mounting amours, like a Don Juan turned weary bitch. Jake and Bill Gorton joined in the drunken camaraderie. Yet the endless rounds of drinks seemed to be accompanied by endless rounds of useless quarrels, and the camaraderie was broken by animosities and malice. There was, nevertheless, a certain measure of fellowship, loyalty, and even gaiety. Cohn was outside it, not merely, because he did not belong but because he seemed too self-centered to participate in friendship. Friendship or not, there is no denying the essential futility of their lives. It was a life without purpose or direction, without intensity or passion, without faith in themselves or their world. Nor did they seem truly to believe in the hedonism by which they lived. It seemed that at the bottom of their hearts there lay such a cold dead despair that they drank in order not to think of it; they drank to wind themselves up, like a clock that must be wound every twenty-four hours. So they got through their days.

Whatever fault may be found, however, with the character of these people, Hemingway reserved his most damning portrait for Cohn. Cohn lacked true identity. His personality was without a core; in place of its center, there was only a sickly ego expressing itself in the spurious martyrdom of the weak and self-pitying. Woman-dominated, he was without the vital maleness which Hemingway, like Lawrence, deems absolutely essential to the true man. There was no true pride, no resistance to Cohn. In his love of Brett, he was childish in his possessiveness and unmanly in his subject pursuit. What a sharply contrasting picture Hemingway has painted of Pedro Romero as he paid suit to Brett by fighting his bull in front of her. A polarity has been established between Cohn, unmanly representative of the lost generation, and the primitive, Pedro Romero. When these two fought, the hard male core of the young bullfighter could not be touched by Cohn's punches, and he reduced Cohn to a whimpering child.

Pedro was exempt from the mal de siècle that beset the others, for his fighting with the bulls brought him into a fundamental relationship with life, which involved the pitting of his maleness against that of the bull. It is a life and death struggle that reveals not only the steal of his young manhood but a certain passion with which he met life -an intensity, a seriousness, a dedicated quality. Pedro had a place in the scheme of existence -and a role to fulfill. With the instinctive sureness of a primitive who need never question his reason for living, he pursued his natural course. And it was this which even Brett came to recognize. There was an absolute center to him. He did not have to drink, he did not have to keep running away. His inner core was brought into a vital active relationship with life. As Jake commented, it is only a bullfighter who lives life to the hilt, bringing to his work all his courage, intelligence, discipline and art.

A purer, more natural kind of love is celebrated in A Farewell to Arms. The novel is a study in disillusionment. Less sustained in movement and less orchestrated than The Sun Also Rises, A Farewell to Arms is a more emotional and subjective novel. It seems to be based upon the memory of a lost love and a lost youth: one's first love, dramatized like that of Romero and Juliet, destroyed by the 'they' that Hemingway in Byronic fashion has cast as the enemy that ever seeks to crush the individual. Although there is no primitive, like Pedro Romero, in this novel, there is, in contrast to the comparatively disillusioned picture of the war, the love itself-tender and idyllic. Glowing with the first flush of the lovers' physical discovery of each other, their love overarches the lovers themselves, who remain essentially passive. It is true that the people in The Sun Also Rises and A Farewell to Arms are world-weary and sophisticated. But they are people who sturdily refuse to be intellectual or aesthetic, as they refuse to be polite or moral. They may well-neigh be called uncivilized. They represent a nostalgic return to the primitive. Lyrically conceived by the author, it is small fire of life dampened by a sense of doom and threatened by the cold rain of death.

It is this twining of sex and death, both fundamental crises of life, that is central to Hemingway's work. Both killing and sexual union are basic primitive experiences in which the male asserts his will and proves his manhood. In the primitive mind, both love and death are surrounded by religious and fearful influences. Because of a sense of danger and evil attending both marriage and death, ceremonies are instituted and taboos and restrictions imposed as safeguards. And Hemingway -defying Christianity's condemnation of killing and its concept of sex as sort of necessary sin -has presented love as a mystic ceremonial experience and killing as a spiritual experience. In a world from which Hemingway has sought to disassociate himself, the only sacred subjects left for him have proved to be love and death -experiences which he has sought to invest with the quality of ancient mysteries.

It would seem, then, that, while Maria is associated with the sun, and the sun generally with life, she is also associated with the Virgin, and the Virgin with the death.

Yet in the last chapter –when all that has gone before has led us painstakingly and inevitably to the destruction of the bridge –the sun is curiously twisted together with death. The scene is the opening of the chapter, just prior to the commencement of the Loyalist attack at dawn, the bombing to serve as a signal for the blowing of the bridge. Jordan, who had always loved the coming of the sun, lay on the pine-needled earth obscured the outline of the bridge. As the bridge shone clear in the morning light, he heard the bombs drop, and he drew along breath, as if to expel the lonely feeling that came with the dealing of death, and he prepared to shoot the sentry. The sentry stood in the road with the sun shining on him. There was no mist on the road now and Robert Jordan saw the man, clearly and sharply, standing there on the road looking up at the sky. The sun shone bright on the trees. Moreover, gently Robert Jordan squeezed the trigger. After the death of the sentry came the wiring of the bridge. With the sound of shots in his ear, suspended under the trestle of the bridge, Jordan worked with a tense quick deliberateness against time, lashing the grenades to the girders. However, for a moment, the noise of the white bubbling stream below him drowned out the war, and looking down he saw a trout nibbling on the chip he had dropped and through the metal of the bridge, he saw the sunlight on the green slope that had been brown but three days ago. It was a green moment of peace that could not be, and it had to yield the twisting of sun and bridge into destruction.

Yet death in this novel is different from death in The Sun Also Rises Death in the Afternoon. In those earlier works, the dominating point of view was that of the matador, because killing was the means of proving one's manhood. The identification was chiefly with the killer; there was a deep fundamental enjoyment, Hemingway said, to be had from killing. In For Whom the Bell Tolls, however, there is an ambiguity of attitude. The novelist here places his hero in the setting of the Spanish Civil

War, mixing up his sense of duty with his usual romantic love situation. In only one instance did Robert Jordan identify himself, partially at least, with the desire to kill. This took place at the scene when Robert Jordan and Agustin, tense and still behind their guns, were watching the enemy cavalry depart. Agustin, speaking of the necessity to kill that was on him 'on a mare in heat', said that there was no stronger thing in life. Jordan, in silent thought, called it the Spanish 'extra sacrament' that, repressed by Christianity, had walled forth in wars and inquisitions; and Jordan admitted that he too and 'all who are soldiers by choice have enjoyed it at some time whether they lie about it or not.' Yet throughout the story Jordan never killed with pleasure but always with reluctance.

Probably, Hemingway's best attempt is his novelette The Old Man And The Sea. When we reach The Old Man And The Sea, we seem to have come a long way from the early works, but there is a pattern into which all of them fall. In The Old Man And The Sea, the fishing is a grinding necessity rather than a sport, and the real subject is a quality of epic endurance. It is true that the old man is the only hero who is not left alone, at the end of the story, with death or despair. He is old, womanless, and humble. Yet in him, we have a blending of the two dominant motifs –the matador and the crucified.

At first glance, it may not seem that what the matador represents is in the old man too. Yet just as the matador pits himself against the bull, so does Santiago pit himself against the great fish; in their killing they achieve a rebellion against death. In this combat, both men must call upon their pride and courage, their skill and knowledge of their craft. Whereas the bullfight terminates with the final sword thrust between the shoulders of the bull, the fight with the fish terminates with the thrusting of the harpoon into his heart. And the old man, his hands lacerated and mushily, raises himself out of his pain to bring down the harpoon, in the same way as the matador Maera in Death in the Afternoon, disregarding his broken wrist, goes in for the sixth time over the horns of the bull. Nevertheless, there are differences. The artificial setting of the bullfight, its spectators, and its ceremony leave one with the sense that this is but violence on exhibit, which is not a natural struggle between man and animal and that the emotions produced scam strained and self-induced. But Santiago's struggle with the fish is natural. As he says, he was born to be a fisherman and the fish was born to be a fish. The killing of fish is an old accepted livelihood. And the setting for Santiago's struggle is the most natural in the world; overhead move the sun and the stars and the moon; beneath sways the sea, la mar; and about the boat move the birds and fish. The sea is the old man's home and the others are his friends and brothers. The old fisherman himself -his skin blotched brown by the friendly sun, his eyes 'the color of the sea', the scars on his hands 'old as erosions in a fishless desert' -is part of this natural universe. It is a complete and closed universe, a friendly one -its Creator neither hostile nor beneficent but mysteriously just. And the old man talks to the fish and birds and the stars just as primitive man might have done long ago.

Yet more remarkable than Santiago's killing of the fish is his suffering. Etched on the reader's mind is the image of the old man as he settled against the wood of the bow -the big fish towing, the cord tight across the old man's back -and took his suffering as it came, telling himself, 'Rest gently now against the wood and think of nothing'. The old man rode gently with the small sea and the hurt of the cord across his back came to him easily and smoothly. The final appearance of Santiago on thewood blend magically into an image of Christ on the cross reminds us of Christ's final show where the suffering is ultimate but the appearance is gentleman Santiago too resembles the same agony of pain with endurance. Then as he was pinned to the bow, dreaming for a few minutes of the lions on the long yellow beach, he woke suddenly with a jerk, the line burning his right hand, his left without feeling. He learned against the line and tried to break it, while it burned his back and cut deeply into his left hand. 'Just then the fish jumped making a great bursting of the ocean ... jumped again and again'. The straining line pulled the old man face down into the slice of dolphin at the bow. He got his head out of the fish, which was nauseating him, and rose, slowly to his knees. Taking the strain with his left hand, he washed the dolphin off his face and left his bleeding right hand trail clean in the salt water, reassuring himself, 'Pain does not matter to a man'. The fish circled slowly, while 'the old man was wet with sweat and tired deep into his bones' and his hands were mushy and he was seeing only in flashes and he was feeling himself go. It was then that he prepared for the kill, pitting 'all his pain and what was left of his strength and his long gone pride' against the agony of the fish. When he thrust and pushed his harpoon into the fish's heart, 'Then the fish came alive, with his death in him, and rose high out of the water showing all his great length and width and all his power and beauty. Then he fell into the water with a crash that sent spray over the old man and all of the skiff'. For a moment after the death of the fish, the tension relaxed, but the pain continued and then the sharks came, 'Aye', he said aloud. There is no translation for this word and perhaps it is just a noise such as a man might make, involuntarily, feeling the nail go through his hands and into the wood. He fought with the sharks through the afternoon, into the evening and the night, until he was almost dead; but the pain of life in his hands and shoulders told him otherwise. He fought until he was weaponless. Then he knew he was beaten and turned the skiff home. The sharks bit into what was left of the great fish, but the old man did not heed them. He was past everything now. Finally sailing into the little harbor, making the boat fast, and stepping ashore, he shouldered the mast and started to climb. It was then that he knew the depth of his tiredness, as he looked back at the head and the white skeleton of the great fish. He climbed again, bearing his mast like a heavy cross, and at the top, he fell and lay for some time with the mast across his shoulder. He got up again. Then reaching his shack, he put the mast against the wall and lay down on his bed. The next morning the boy found him -his face down on the newspapers with his arms out straight and the palms of his hands out.

Yet that afternoon the old man was dreaming of the lions on the white beach of Africa. The dream may represent, as Philip Young has suggested, not only a nostalgic return to the strength of one's youth but also desire for immortality -like the meaning of the frozen leopard on the summit of Kilimanjaro. Despite the suffering and seeming defeat of the old man, the final effect is that of a triumph which is invested not with the violent ritualized quality of the bullfights of Death in the Afternoon or the uneasily insistent and belligerent note of Green Hills of Africa, but with a warm autumnal glow. The old man beating off the sharks is like life rebelling against death -as though the old man and the great fish who are lashed together and steering as one toward home, just as earlier they had been bound by the 'pain of life', have become the symbol of life; while the sharks have become the symbol of death which must be resisted even though it will win.

Combined with this triumph is tenderness not usually found in Hemingway's work. For all of Hemingway's glorifying of love between man and woman, too much of the author seemed involved, as Edmund Wilson and Philip Young have noted, with a repudiation of woman. But now in the relation between man and boy, Hemingway achieves a new gentleness. This turning to male companionships seems characteristically American, recalling the paired Huck Finn and Jim, Nattty Bumppo and Chingachgook, Ismael and Queequeg. Curiously, with the exception of Ismael, they are all variations primitives. And in Santiago, Hemingway has created as fine a primitive as the twentieth century has revealed, one who seems worthy of comparison with Mark Twain's Huck Finn or Jim. But the old man is more richly endowed than most primitives: bearing the name of Saint James, who was a fisherman and martyr, he strangely unites the matador and the crucified, the symbols that reveal Hemingway's gospel of action.

Hemingway's indirect way of narration is at his best in his short stories in which he has often, within small compass, successfully evoked a sense of the tragic through the overtones of his prose. There is an impersonal quality in his tales, and a sustained picture, which he cannot maintain in his longer works.

In the final analysis, we find that Hemingway all through insisted on action, which is his central philosophy. In life, he gives prime importance to action. Action emerges from self-consciousness, which is an innate quality. The stories of Hemingway's novels have been spun out of the fabrics of this perennial philosophy; and this acts as a healing balm on the jaded spirit of the broken man of our day. The substance of most of Hemingway's work is made brilliant by a studied lucidity that constitutes the most important side of his achievement in contemporary American literature. His closely written and unsentimental style and his mastery of dialogue have led critics to raise him high among all living writers.

Bibliography

PRIMARY SOURCES

Hemingway, Ernest: The Sun Also Rises, Granada Publishing Ltd., Granada, 1976.

____________ A Farewell to Arms, Triad/Panther Books, Frogmore, St. Albanas, Herts AL2 2NF, 1977.

____________ To Have and Have Not, Triad/Panther Books, Frogmore, St. Albanas, Herts AL2 2NF, 1977.

____________ For Whom the Bell Tolls, Triad/Panther Books, Frogmore, St. Albanas, Herts AL2 2NF, 1977.

____________ The Old Man And The Sea, Surjeet Publications, New Delhi, 1977

____________ Death in the Afternoon, Triad/Panther Books, Frogmore, St. Albanas, Herts AL2 2NF, 1977.

____________ Across the River and into Trees, Triad/Panther Books, Frogmore, St. Albanas, Herts AL2 2NF, 1978.

____________ The End of Something, Triad/Panther Books, Frogmore, St. Albanas, Herts AL2 2NF, 1979.

____________ Fathers and Sons, Triad/Panther Books, Frogmore, St. Albanas, Herts AL2 2NF, 1980.

SECONDARY SOURCES

Atkins, J.A. The Art of Ernest Hemingway, His Work and Personality, Macmillan, London, 1952.

Allen, Walter Tradition and Dream, Penguin, Harmondsworth, 1979.

Arnold, L.R. High on the Wild with Hemingway, The Caxton Printers Ltd., U.S.A., 1969.

Asselineau, R. (ed.) The Literary Reputation of Hemingway in Europe, New York University Press, New York, 1965.

Baker, Carlos Hemingway, The Writer as Artist, Princeton University Press, Princeton, 1963.

____________ Hemingway and His Critics, Hill and Wang, New York, 1961.

Bates, H.E. The Modern Short Story : A Critical Survey, Oxford University Press, London, 1943.

Beach, J.W. The Twentieth Century Novel : Studies in Technique, New York University Press, New York, 1932.

Barrett, W. Irrational Man, Oxford University Press, New York, 1962.

Benson, Jackson, J. Hemingway, The Writer's Art of Self Defense, University of Minnesota Press, Minneapolis, 1969.

Beger, Peter, In Berger, Peter and Kellner, The Homeless Mind. New York: Vintage Books, 1974.

Burgum, E.B. The Novel and the World's Dilemma, New York University Press, New York, 1947.

Cargill, Oscar Intellectual America : Ideas on the March, New York University Press, New York, 1941.

Canby, H.S. and Others Literary History of the United States, Amerind Publishing Co. Pvt. Ltd., New Delhi, 1963.

Cunliffe, Marcus The Literature of the United States, Penguin Books Ltd., Great Britain, 1961.

Daiches, David The Novel and the Modern World, The University of Chicago Press, Chicago, 1967.

Emerson, R.W. Essays, Eurassia Publishing House, New Delhi, New Delhi, 1965.

Fenton, C.A. The Apprenticeship of Ernest Hemingway: The Early Years, Oxford University Press, New York, 1954.

Frohock, W.M. The Novel of Violence in America, 1920-1950, Mc Caffery, New York, 1950.

Hartwick, Harry Foreground of American Fiction, New York University Press, New York, 1934.

Hatcher, Harlan Creating the Modern American Novel, Oxford University Press. New York, 1935.

Heinemann Existentialism and the Modern Predicament (3rd edition), Atma and Charles Black, London, 1950.

Hoffman, F.J. The Modern Novel in America 1900-1950, Chicago University Press, Chicago, 1951.

Hutchins, R.M. Gateway to the Great Books, Britannica, INC, London, 1963.

Karzin, Alfred On Native Grounds : An Interpretation of Modern Prose Literature, Reynal & Hitchcock, New York, 1942.

Kettle, Arnold An Introduction to the English Novel, arrow Books Ltd., London, 1951.

Mc Caffery, J.K.M. Ernest Hemingway :The Man and His Work, The World Publishing Co., Cleveland, 1950.

Muir, Edwin The Structure of the Novel, Allied Publishers Pvt. Ltd., Bombay, 1966.

Orvis, Mary The Art of Writing Fiction, New York University Press, New York, 1948.

Ross, Lillian Portrait of Hemingway, Semon & Sahuster, New Jersey, 1961.

Rovit, Earl H. Ernest Hemingway, Macmillan & Co., Twayne, 1963.

Shapiro, C. (ed) Twelve Original Essays on Great American Novels, Detroit, New York, 1958.

Spiller, Robert E. The Cycle of American Literature, The American Library, U.S.A., 1963.

Straumann, H. American Literature in the Twentieth Century, Grey Arrow ion, Oxford, 1962.

Wangenknecht, Edward Cavalcade of the American Novel, Oxford and IBH Publishing Co., Calcutta, 1969.

Watt, Ian The Rise of the Novel, Chatto and Windus, London, 1960.

Weeks, Robert P. (ed.) Hemingway, Princeton University Press, Princeton, 1962.

West, Ray B. Jr., The Art of Modern Fiction, Oxford and Stallman, R.W. University Press, New York, 1949.

West, Paul The Paul Modern Novel, Hutchinson and Co. Ltd., London, 1967.

Young, Philip Ernest Hemingway, University of Minnesota Presss, New York, 1959.

____________ Ernest Hemingway : A Reconsideration, Pennsylvania State University Press, Pennsylvania, 1966.

JOURNALS

Adams, J. Donald "Ernest Hemingway", English Journal, XXVIII, 1939, pp. 87-94.

____________ "The Shape of Books to Come", English Journal, XXX, 1941, pp. 325-345.

Adams, Richard P. "Sunrise Out of the Waste Land", Tulane studies in English, IX, 1959, pp. 119-31.

Aldridge, John W. "Hemingway :The Etiquette of the Berserk", Mandrake, II, Autumn-Winter, 1954-55, pp. 331-41.

Alsop, Joseph "A Cuban Visit with Hemingway", New York Herald Tribune, Mar. 9, 1960, p. 18.

Backman, Melvin "Hemingway: The Matador and the Crucified", Modern Fiction Studies, Aug. 1955, pp. 2-11.

Baker, Carlos "The Hard Trade of Mr. Hemingway", Delphian Quarterly, XXIII, July 1940, pp. 12-17.

__________ "Hemingway's Wastelanders", Virginia Quarterly Review, XXVIII, Summer, 1952, pp. 373-92.

Barea, Arturo "Not Spain But Hemingway", Horizon, II, May 1941, pp. 350-61.

Barnes, Lois L. "The Helpless Hero of Ernest Hemingway!" Science and Society, XVII, 1953, pp. 1-25.

Beach, J.W. "How Do You Like It Now, Gentlemen?", Sewanee Review, LXI, Spring, 1951, pp. 311-18.

Beaver, Joseph "Technique in Hemingway", College English, XIV, March, 1953, pp. 325-28.

Brown, Deming "Hemingway in Russia", American Quarterly, V, 1953, pp.143-56.

Burnam, Tom "Primitivism and Masculinity in the work of Ernest Hemingway", Modern Fiction Studies, I, Aug., 1955, pp.20-24.

Carpenter, F.I. "Hemingway Achieves the Fifth Dimension", Publications of Modern Language Association, LXIX, Sept., 1954, pp. 711-18.

Colvert, James B. "Ernest Hemingway's Morality in Action", American Literature, XXVII, Nov. 1955, pp. 372-85.

Cooke, Alistair "Hemingway : Master of the Mid-west Vernacular", Manchester Guardian Weekly, Nov. 11, 1954, p. 7.

Cooperman, Stanley "Hemingway and Old Age: Santiago as Priest of Time", College English, Vol. 27, No. 3, December, 1965, pp. 215-20.

Cousins, Norman "For Whom the Bells Ring", Saturday Review of Literature, XLII, Aug. 22, 1959, p. 18.

Cowley, Malcolm "Ernest Hemingway :A Farewell to Spain", New Republic, LXXIII, Nov. 30, 1932, pp. 76-77.

D'Agostino, Nemi "The Later Hemingway", Sewanee Review, LXVIII, Summer, 1960, pp.482-93.

Daniel, Robert "Hemingway and His Heroes", Queen's Quarterly, LIV, Winter, 1947-48, pp.471-85.

Dewing, Arthur "The Mistake about Hemingway", North American review, CCXXXII,1931, pp. 364-71.

Freedman, Richard "Hemingway's Spanish Civil War Dispatches", Texas Studies in Literature and Language, I, Summer, 1959, pp. 171-80.

Friedman, Norman "Criticism and the Novel : Hardy, Hemingway, Crane, Woolf, Conrad", Antioch Review, XVIII, Fall, 1958, pp. 343-70.

Friedrich, Otto "Ernest Hemingway : Joy Through Strength", American Scholar, XXVI, Autumn, 1957, pp. 518-30.

Frohock, W.M. "Hemingway and Mark Twain", Accent, XIV, Summer, 1954, pp. 199-206.

Gordon, Caroline "Notes on Hemingway and Kafka", Sewanee Review, LVII, 1959, pp. 215-26.

Guttmann, Alan "Mechanized Doom : Ernest Hemingway and the Spanish Civil War", Massachusetts Review, I, May, 1960, pp. 541-61.

Halliday, E.M. "Hemingway's Ambiguity : Symbolism and Irony", American Literature, XXVIII, March, 1956, pp. 1-22.

__________ "Hemingway's Hero", University of Chicago Magazine, XLV, May, 1953, pp. 10-14.

__________ "Hemingway's In Our Time", Explicator, VII, March, 1949, p. 35.

__________ "Hemingway's Narrative Perspective", Sewanee Review, LX, Spring, 1952, pp. 202-18.

Holmes, John C. "Existentialism and the Novel : Notes and Questions", Chicago Review, XVIII, summer, 1959, pp. 144-51.

Jameson, Storm "The Craft of the Novelist", English Review, LVIII, 1934, pp.144-51.

MaClennan, Joshua "Ernest Hemingway and His Audience", Michigan Alumnus Quarterly Review, LIX, Summer, 1953, pp. 335-40.

O'Faolain, Sean "The Vanishing Hero", Studies in Novelists of the Twenties, London, 1956, pp. 135-65.

Paul, Eliot "Hemingway and the Critics", Sturday Review of Literature, XVII, Nov. ^, 1937, pp. 3-4.

Phillips, W. "Ernest Hemingway", Paris Review, XVIII, Spring, 1958, pp. 61-82.

Trilling, Lionel "Hemingway and His Critics", Partisan Review, VI, Winter, 1939, pp. 52-60.

Sylvester, Bickford "Hemingway's Extended Vision: The Old Man And The Sea", PMLA, LXXXI. March 1966, p. 130-38.

____________ "The Cuban Context of The Old Man The Sea", The Cambridge Companion to Ernest Hemingway. (Ed.) Donaldson, Scott. UK: Cambridge University Press, 1996, 243-68.

Wells R. Arvin: "A Rural of Transfiguration: The Old Man And The sea", The University Review, Vol. XXX, Winter 1963, P. 95-101.

Wyruck, Green D. "Hemingway and Bergson : the Elan Vital", Modern Fiction Studies, I, August, 1955, pp. 17-19.

REFERENCES FOR GENERAL STUDIES

Oswald Spengler The Decline of the West, 2 Vols., New York University Press, New York, 1926.

Arnold Toynbee A Study of History, Oxford University Press, New York, 1957.

Roderick Seidenber Posthistoric Man, Boston University Press, Boston, 1957.

Friedrich Juenger The Failure of Technology, Chicago University Press, Chicago, 1956.

Hannah Arendt The Human Condition, Chicago University Press, Chicago, 1958.

Erich Kahler The Tower and the Abyss, New York University Press, New York, 1957.

Sigmund Freud Civilization and Its Discontents, Oxford University Press, London, 1955.

Theodore Reik Of Love and Lust, Oxford University Press, New York, 1957.

Alain Touraine The Self-production of Society. (Trans.) Coltman, Derek Chicago: University of Chicago Press, 1973.

Walter Kaufmann (ed.) Existentialism from Dostoyevsky to Sartre, New York University Press, New York, 1957.

Robert Bretall (ed) A Kierkegaard Anthology, Princeton University Press, Princeton, 1951.

Lionel Trilling Freud and the Crisis of Our culture, Boston University Press, Boston, 1955.

Mario Praz. The Hero in Eclipse in Victorian Fiction New York University Press, New York, 1956.

Aldous Huxley The Letters of D.H. Lawrence, Macmillan & Co., London, 1956.

James Joyce Ulysses, Oxford University Press, New York, 1946.

Thomas Mann The Magic Mountain, New York, 1955.

Hermann Hesse Steppenwolf, Oxford University Press, New York, 1929.

Jean Paul Nausea Conn., Norfolk, 1958.

Ortega Y. Gasset The Dehumanization of Art, New York University Press, New York, 1956.

Karl Jaspers Man in the Modern Age, New York University Press, New York, 1957.

Leslie Fiedler An End of Innocence, Boston University Press, Boston, 1955.

D. H. Lawrence Studies in Classic American Literature, New York University Press, New York, 1951.

George Santayana Character and Opinion, Oxford University Press, New York, 1955.

Jacques Maritain Reflections on America, New York University Press, New York, 1958.

Mark Twain The Adventure of Huckleberry Finn, New York University Press, New York, 1953.

F. W. Dupee Henry James, New York University Press, New York, 1956.

Frederick Allen Only Yesterday, New York University Press, New York, 1931.

Theodore Dreiser An American Tragedy, New York University Press, New York, 1925.

John Dos Passos Three Soldiers, New York University Press, New York, 1932.

Thomas Wolfe Look Homeward, Angel, Oxford University Press, New York, 1929.

Edmund Wilson The American Earthquake, Penguin Books, New York, 1958.

Notes and References

(Endnotes)

1. Quoted by Paul Darcy Boles: "The Vision Then and Now", in Granville Hicks, ed., The Living Novel, New York, 1957, p.31.
2. Flannery O'Connor: "The Fiction Writer and this Country", in The Living Novel, New York, 1961, P. 162.
3. Lionel Trilling: The Opposing Self, New York, 1955, p. x.
4. Wright Morris:"The Territory Ahead" in The Living Novel, Op.cit. p.146.
5. Richard Chase: The Democratic Vista, New York, 1958, p.30.
6. Paul Radin: The Trickster, Chato & Windus, London, 1956, p.200.
7. Arthur Mizener: "The Lost Generation", quoted in Modern American Literature, Higginbotharas(P) Ltd., Mount Road, Madras, 1958, p.113.
8. Ibid., p. 118.
9. Quoted in American Literature, "The Lost Generation", by Arthur Mizener, Higginbothan (P) Ltd., Madras-2, 1958, p.119.

10. Ibid., p. 120.
11. Ernest Hemingway: "Now I Lay Me" The Fifth Column and The First Forty-nine Stories, New York, 1938, p. 461.
12. Andre Maurois; "Ernest Hemingway", Hemingway and His Critics, Ed. Carlos Baker, Hill and Wang, New York, 1961, p.41.
13. Ibid., p.42.
14. Ibid., p.43.
15. Ibid., P.44.
16. Quoted in Philip Young: Ernest Hemingway, London, Macmillan, 1952, p.48.
17. Carlos Baker: op. cit., p.46.
18. The Fifth Column and the First Fortynine Stories, New York, 1938, P. vii.
19. Carlos Baker: op. cit., p. 48.
20. Ibid., p. 49.
21. Ibid., p. 49.
22. Ibid., p. 50.
23. Ibid., p. 50.
24. Philip Young: op. cit., p. 36.
25. Hemingway: 'The Short Happy Life of Francis Macomber.
26. Carlos Baker, op. cit., p. 51.
27. Hemingway: 'The Short Happy Life of Francis Macomber.
28. Ibid., p. 52.
29. John Brown: Panorama de la literature contemporaine aux Etats-Unis, Paris: Gallimard, 1954, p. 129.
30. Marcus Guniliffe: cited, The Literature of the United States, Penguin, 1966, p. 287.

31. A.G. Paranjpe: In Search of Identity, John Viley &Sons, Ahalsted Press Book, New York, 1975, p.1.

32. Cleanth Brooks: 'Eve's Awakening', Modern Judgement, ed.Alan Rudrum, Macmillan & Co. Ltd., London, 1968, p. 10.

33. The Holy Bible, The Old Testament, 'The Book of Job', New York, 1959, P. 540.

34. Ibid., p. 552.

35. George E. Dimock Jr.: 'The Name of Odyssey', ed. George Steiner and Robert Fagles, Homer, INC., Englewood Cliffs, 1962, p. 106.

36. Christopher Marlowe: Doctor Faustus, Doaba House, Delhi, 1982, p. 102.

37. William Shakespeare: Macbeth, Act, I, Scene, III, 50, Magpie Books Ltd, London, 1992, p. 847.

38. Darshan Singh Maini: 'Henry James', The Portrait of a Lady :An Assessment, Oxford University Press, Calcutta, 1977, p. 34.

39. Heinrich Stroumman : American Literature in the Twentieth Century, Arrows Books Ltd., New York, 1962, p.45.

40. Grosset and Dunlap: Dodsworth, New York, 1929, p. 225.

41. Ibid. , p. 362.

42 American Literature in the Twentieth Century, op. cit., p.45.

43. Doss Passos: Rosinate to the Road Again, Brands & Brands, New York, 1922, p. 53.

44. Rosinate to the Road Again, op. cit., p.53.

45. Ibid., p.61.

46. Doss Passos: The Ground We Stand on, Marcourt, Brace and Co., New York, 1941, p.12.

47. American Literature in the Twentieth Century, op. cit., p.54.

48. Ibid., p. 55.

49. T.S.Eliot: "The Waste Land" III, The Fire Sermon, Selected Poems, Fabre and Fabre, London, p. 66.

50. The Waste Land, II A Game of Chess, op. cit. p. 66.

51. Ibid. p. 67.

52. Philip Larkin: "Wants", The golden Treasury, Oxford University Press, Calcutta, 1978, p. 556.

53. Heinrich Straumann: American Literature in the Twentieth Century, Grey Arrow Edition, New York, 1962, p. 116.

54. Abbe de Prett: "De Colonieset de la Revolution actuelle de l Amerique", Literary History of United States, Amerind Publishing Co. Pvt. Ltd., Delhi, 1972, p. 207.

55. Edgar Quinet, Reve des Deux Mones, op. cit., p.214.

56. Siegfried Sassoon: 'Counter Attack', Mundra, A history of English Literature, 1982, p. 608.

57. Lois Mac Neice: "Prayer Before Birth"' The Golden Treasury, Oxford University Press, Calcutta, 1978, p.518.

58. William Barrett: "What is Existentialism?", Partisan Review Series, No. 2, New York, 1947, p. 12.

59. Conard Ficken: "Hanging Gardens", Selected Poems, Charles Scribner's Sons, New York, London, 1929, p. 350.

60. W.B.Yeats: "The Second Coming", Selected Poetry, ed. A. Norman Jeffares, Pub. A Norman Jeffares, Macmillan &Co. Ltd., London, 1962, p. 99.

61. Rubaiyat of Umar Khayyam of Naishapur, Translated by Edward Fitzgerald, Rupa &Co., New Delhi, 1980, p. 16.

62. Rubaiyat of Umar Khayyam of Naishapur, Translated by Edward Fitzgerald, The Golden Treasury, Oxford University Press, Calcutta, 1978, p. 329.

63. Mathew Arnold: 'Dover Beach', Palgrave's Golden Treasury, Oxford University Press, Calcutta, 1978, p. 365.

64. Hennery Miller: Tropic of Cancer, Granada Publishing Ltd., New York, 1980, p. 45.

65. Ibid., p. 47.

66. Henry Miller: Black Spring, Grove Press, New York, 11963, p. 96.

67. Ibid., p. 96.

68. Ernest Hemingway: A Farewell to Arms, Triad/ Panther Books Frogmore, St. Albans, Herts AL 2 2 NE, P. 57.

69. Ernest Hemingway: A Farewell to Arms, op.cit. p. 57.

70. Ibid., pp 26-27.

71. Ibid., p. 57.

72. Ibid., p. 57.

73. Ibid., p. 28.

74. Ernest Hemingway: A Farewell to Arms, P. 70.

75. Ibid., p. 85.

76. G.B.Shaw: Arms and the Man, Surjeet Book Depot, New Delhi, 1979, pp. 75-76.

77. Ernest Hemingway: A Farewell to Arms, pp. 166-67.

78. Jackson J. Benson: Hemingway –The Writer's Art of Self-Defense, University of Minnesota Press, Minneapoli, p. 106.

79. Ian Ousby: An Introduction to Fifty American Novels, Pan Books, London, 1980, p. 240.

80. Hemingway: To Have and Have Not, Penguin Books Ltd., England, 1977, pp. 90-91.

81. Ibid., pp. 137-38.

82. Hemingway: For Whom the Bell Tolls, Triad/Panther

Books Frogmore, St. Albanas, Herts, AL2 2NF, 1977, p. 70.

83. Ibid., p. 71.
84. Hemingway: For Whom the Bell Tolla, p. 145.
85. Ibid., p .234.
86. Ibid., p. 307.
87. Ibid., p. 235.
88. Ibid., pp. 405-406.
89. R.S.Thomas: "Here", The Golden Treasury, ed. Palgrave, F.T., Oxford University Press, Calcutta, 1978, p. 538.
90. Tennessee Williams: A Street Car Named Desire, Penguin Books Ltd., England, 1981, p. 169.
91. Robert Frost: "Stopping by Woods on a Snowy Evening", A Book of Poems, National Publishing House, Delhi, 1975, p. 69.
92. Matthew Arnold: "Switzerland", The Golden Treasury, op. cit., p. 364.
93. Hemingway: To Have and Have Not, Penguin Books Ltd., England, 1977, p. 176.
94. Hemingway: To Have and Have Not, pp. 177-78.
95. Hemingway: For Whom the Bell Tolls, Triad/Panther Books, Frogmore, St. Albanas, Herts, 1976, p. 69.
96. Hemingway: For Whom the Bell Tolls, p.181.
97. Ibid., p. 139.
98. Ibid., pp. 127-28.
99. Ibid., pp. 342-43.
100. Ibid., p. 411.
101. Hemingway: The Old Man and the Sea, Surjeet Publications, Delhi, 1977, p. 6.
102. Ibid., p. 12.
103. Ibid., p. 12.

104. Arthur Miller: The Death of a Salesman, The Viking Press, New York, 1949, p. 138.
105. Hemingway: The Old Man and the Sea, pp. 52-53.
106. T.S.Eliot: "The Love Song of J. Alfred Purfrock", Selected Poems, Faber and Fabre, London, 1980, p. 11.
107. Hemingway: The Old Man and the Sea, p. 82.
108. Ibid., p. 103.
109. Hemingway: The Old Man and the Sea, p. 127.
110. Jackson J. Benson: Hemingway: The Writers Art of Self Defense, University of Minnesota Press, Minneapolis, 1945, p. 44.
111. Middleton: The Changeling, Penguin Books Ltd., Harmondsworth, 1978, p. 61.
112. T.S.Eliot: 'The Love Song of J.Alfred Prufrock', Selected Poems, Fabre & Fabre, London, 1980, p. 14.
113. Shelly: To A Skylark, R. Dayal, O.U.P., Faraday House, p. 243.
114. Shakespeare: Measure for Measure, Act III, Sc. I, 31-34, Magpie Books Ltd, London, p. 83.
115. Ibid., Act III, Sc. I, 82-83, p. 84.
116. Shakespeare: Antony and Cleopatra, Act IV, Sc. XII, 98-101. Magpie Books Ltd, London, p. 1005.
117. W. H. Auden: "The Shield of Achilles", Golden Treasury, ed. Palgrave, O.U.P., Calcutta, 1978, p. 513.
118. Will Durant: cited, The Story of Philosophy, New York, 1957, p. 513.
119. Ibid., p. 416.
120. Hemingway: Death in the Afternoon, Triad / Panther Books, Frogmore, St. Albanes, 1977, p. 234.
121. Ibid., pp. 206-07.
122. Hemingway: The Sun Also Rises, Triad / Panther Books, Frogmore, St. Albanes, 1977, p. 96.

123. Ibid., p. 206.
124. Ibid., p. 206.
125. Hemingway: A Farewell to Arms, Triad / Panther Books, Frogmore, St. Albanes Herts, P. 44.
126. Ibid., p. 113.
127. Ibid., p. 114.
128. Ibid.
129. Ibid.
130. Hemingway: A Farewell to Arms, p. 227.
131. Ibid., p. 234.
132. Hemingway: For Whom the Bell Tolls, Triad / Panther Books, St. Frogmore, 1976, p. 55.
133. Ibid., p. 86.
134. Hemingway: For Whom the Bell Tolls, p. 139.
135. Ibid., p. 275.
136. Ibid., p. 276.
137. Ibid., p. 283.
138. Ibid., p. 405.
139. Ibid., p. 407.
140. Ibid., p. 409.
141. Dylan Thomas: "Death and Entrance", A History of English Literature, Mundra, Prakash Book Depoty, Delhi, 1982, p. 627.
142. Ezra Pound: "Selwyn Mauberely", Literary History of United States, Ed. Spillar and others, Amerinel Publishing Co. Pvt. Ltd., New Delhi, 1969, p. 1338.
143. T.S.Eliot: "The Love Song of J. Alfred Prufrock", Selected Poems:, p. 12.
144. William Barrett: Irrational Man, Viking, New York, 1962, p. 16.
145. John Clare, "I am", Golden Treasury, Ed. Palgrave, Oxford University Press, Calcutta, 1980, p. 319.

146. William Barrett: Irrational Man, p. 31.
147. Quoted by Eric Bentley: The Playwright As Thinkers, New York, 1946, P. 195.
148. Striendberg: "The Father", Classics of Modern Theatre, ed. Alvin B. Kernan, Penguin, New York, 1965, p. 108.
149. Ted Hughes: "Hawk Roosting", The Golden Treasury, ed. Palgrave, Oxford University Press, Calcutta, 1970, P. 565.
150. Spiller: The Cycle of American Literature, The New American Library, New York, 1963, p. 205.
151. Quoted by William Barrett: Irrational Man, po.cit., p. 44.
152. T.S.Eliot: "The Love Song of J. Alfred Prufrock", Selected Poems, P. 11.
153. T.S.Eliot: "The Waste Land", 'The Burial of the Dead', Selected Poems, p. 63.
154. Ibid., p. 51.
155. Hemingway: The Sun Also Rises, Triad/Panther Books Ltd., England, 1980, p. 239.
156. Ibid., p. 247.
157. D.G.Rossetti: "A Superscription", The Golden Treasury, op. cit., p. 371.
158. Spiller: The Cycle of American Literature, op. cit., p. 205.
159. The Sun also Rises, op. cit., p. 247.
160. Hemingway: A Farewell to arms, Triad/Panther Books, St. Albans, 1977, p., 31.
161. Ibid., pp. 26-27.
162. Ibid., p. 44.
163. Ibid., p. 69.
164. Ibid., p. 85.

165. The Cycle of American Literature, op. cit., pp. 205-06.
166. Hemingway: A Farewell to Arms, p. 236.
167. Hemingway: For Whom the Bell Tolls, p. 206.
168. Ibid., p. 148.
169. Ibid., p. 148.
170. Conor Gruise O'Brien: Camus, Wm. Collins Sons &Co. Ltd., London, 1970, p. 34.
171. Ibid., p. 39.
172. Ibid., p. 41.
173. Hemingway: For Whom the Bell Tolls, p. 327.
174. Ibid., p. 408.
175. The Cycle of American Literature, op. cit., pp. 206-07
176. Samuel Beckett: Waiting for Godot, Fabre and Fabre, London, 1979, p. 79.
177. Quoted by E. Hemingway: For Whom the Bell Tolls, op. cit., p. 5.
178. The Old Man And The Sea, op. cit., p. 25.
179. Ibid., p. 17.
180. T.S.Eliot: "Gerontion" Selected poems, p.37.
181. Samuel Beckett: op. cit., p. 41.
182. Hemingway: The Old Man And The Sea, Surjeet Publications, Delhi, 1977, p. 29.
183. Ibid., p. 29.
184. Ibid., p. 37.
185. The Old Man And The Sea, op. cit., p. 25.
186. Ibid., p. 25.
187. Ibid., p. 94.
188. Ibid., p. 81.
189. Ibid., p. 91.

190. Stanley Cooperman, "Hemingway and Old Age: Santiago as Priest of Time", College English, Vol. 27, No. 3, December, 1965, p. 219.

191. Bickford Sylvester: "The Cuban Context of The Old Man And The Sea", The Cambridge Companion to Ernest Hemingway. (Ed.) Donaldson, Scott. UK: Cambridge University Press, 1996, P. 245.

192. Bickford Sylvester: "Hemingway's Extended Vision: The Old Man And The Sea", PMLA, LXXXI. March, 1966, p. 132

193. Peter Beger: In Berger, Peter and Kellner, The Homeless Mind. New York: Vintage Books,1974, P. 91.

194. Ibid., p. 91.

195. Alain Touraine: The Self-production of Society. (Trans.) Coltman, Derek Chicago: University of Chicago Press, 1973, p. 26.

196. Ibid., p. 26.

197. Arvin Wells R.: "A Rural of Transfiguration: The Old Man And The sea", The University Review, Vol. XXX, Winter 1963, P. 95-101.

198. Ibid., p. 95.

199. The Old Man And The Sea, op. cit., p. 116.

200. Ibid., p. 120.

201. Ibid., p. 121.

202. Samuel Beckett: op. cit., p. 80.

203. T.S.Eliot: 'Catholicism and the International Order', Selected Prose, Ed. John Hayward, Penguin, 1963, p. 197.

204. W.B.Yeats: 'The Second Coming', Selected Poems, p. 4.

205. Conrad Aiken: "Preludes to Attitude", Twentieth Century American Poetry, The Modern Library, Random House, New York, 1944, p.227.

206. Matthew Arnold: "Dover Beach", Golden Treasury, Oxford University Press, Calcutta, 1978, p. 1962.
207. Hienrich Straumann: American Literature in the Twentieth Century, Grey Arrow ion, London, 1962, p. 125.
208. Ibid., p. 125.
209. Hemingway: For Whom the Bell Tolls, Triad/Panther Books, St. Albanas, 1976, p. 405.
210. Hemingway: The Old Man And The Sea, Surjeet Publications, Delhi, 1977, p.83.
211. American Literature in the Twentieth Century, op. cit., p.125.
212. Hemingway: For Whom the Bell Tolls, p. 408.
213. Alfred Kazin: On Native Grounds: An Interpretation of Modern American Prose Literature, Renynal & Hitchcock, New York, 1942, p. 31.

Index